Where Fortunes Lie

and other stories

Moira Harris

Where Fortunes Lie

Pre-determined, beyond our control, within self-fulfilling prophecies, accidental, or at the mercy of chance and luck?

In her first published collection of short stories, Moira Harris explores the roles that fortune, luck and chance may play in our lives. Birth, death, love, health, family, the people we meet, being in the wrong or right place at the wrong or right time, our ambitions, our relationships – all are woven into the human condition and subjected to the lottery of life. No matter how organised, conscientious, loving and caring we are, how much control, if any, do we really have?

For Steve

Contents

Enough is enough

Decluttering will revolutionise her life. Bring order and simplicity to her mind, her body her spirit. That's what the experts at *loveselfcare.com* had proclaimed as Alice had scrolled through the website. Dipping her digestive biscuit into the mug of green tea beside the keyboard – she'll surrender her usual milky coffee to the shrine of physical wellness but surrendering the biscuit is unthinkable – she had observed the highly polished faces with matching smiles and read their ecstatic testimonies.

'loveselfcare saved me from drowning in a sea of memories and detritus that was simply harming rather than helping me' – Jayne, Huddersfield

'I had no idea how big my house was until I decluttered with the help of loveselfcare. My family was being suffocated by stuff that had become invisible to them. Now we can all breathe again – it's wonderful!' – Barbara, Kettering

'The loveselfcare programme is so easy to follow. My home now feels like a blank canvas anticipating what is to come. I haven't yet missed a single thing that I gave to the charity store and the recycling centre!' Carol, Slough

Alice was never particularly aware of accumulating to excess until the subtle hints chiselled their way into her thoughts. Living alone, she's created her own system for knowing where things are, even if they're not necessarily in what other people would consider the obvious place.

It seems perfectly sensible to Alice to store magazines and newspapers in the washing basket. And what is wrong with using the spare bedroom as an art studio? There is still a single bed in there - albeit covered with a sheet of MDF to provide a drying surface – and with advanced warning, she can still have a guest to stay. Provided they don't object to the smell of white spirit and adhesive. *loveselfcare* would undoubtedly recommend it being used as a personal shrine, an area dedicated to meditation, mindfulness and yoga. Perhaps if she'd been more mindful, she'd have spread the protective plastic sheeting she bought a year ago across the floor before she spilled red acrylic paint on the cream carpet.

Her sister had first mentioned the claustrophobia-inducing tendencies of the house when she had invited herself to stay with Alice last Spring. Since then, it is always referred to in their weekly phone calls to one another. Alice ignores her sister's interrogation about whether the two bikes – the new one is a replacement for the other one that has a flat tyre and bent handlebars after a collision with a mobility scooter – have been removed from the hallway, whether it is necessary to have so many pictures on the walls and how it is possible to eat at a dinner table buried beneath bills, flyers, correspondence and goodness knows what else. After every call, Alice reminds herself that she does love her sister but also acknowledges the obsessive and snobbish qualities her younger sibling was born with.

It was the collapse of the three stacks of books, none of which could find a home on her congested shelves, that nudged Alice towards taking stock of her household contents. Each stack was as tall as her and she is a tall woman. Had she been shorter, she wouldn't have been standing on tiptoe and placing a recently read Booker Prize winning novel on top of one of the precarious columns. Nor would the entire arrangement have crumpled in slow motion, as an old industrial chimney does when it's blown up, and entirely buried Rasputin, her extremely disgruntled and perplexed cat.

The instructions on the website had been so convincing and seemed so straightforward.

'With loveselfcare.com you will use the FULL technique to ask your senses to decide if an object is Functional or Useful or Loved or Looked at. One answer YES for any of these questions and the object is for keeping. Otherwise, it should be consigned to one of the four large bags that you will label RECYCLE, REGIFT, REASSIGN or RETURN. There is one final destination and that is

RUBBISH. We hope, however, that you will have very little need to make that journey.'

Alice's transformational weekend had got off to a very promising start. Yesterday morning she'd focused on her small bathroom in the hope that it would be a manageable challenge with which to begin. According to the minimalist pundits, this space simply required jettisoning ancient bottles of unused beauty products and out of date prescription medicines. She hasn't yet reached the age when women are chastised into consuming either of these aids to prop up their self-esteem and their gravity-compliant skin.

Reaching into the cupboard beneath her washhand basin, her fingers became stuck in an amalgam of tiny rectangular hotel soaps which had escaped from their packaging and now lay congealed on top of a John le Carré novel. She'd enjoyed reading the book in the bath last winter and assumed she'd lent it to a friend at work.

Body scrubs, incense sticks, unusually scented moisturisers, pumice stones and face clothes – all forming a surprisingly enormous, dusty stockpile of unused Christmas presents – gave themselves up to her searching touch. Alice had realised her world was very different from that of the decluttering experts as she pushed this hoard in among the selection of rusty razor blades, scented candles, pot pourri, sea shells, driftwood, pebbles, dental floss, out-of-date sun cream and cryptic crossword compilations already spread across the tiled floor. Depositing it all in the bin bags flagged with their large, handwritten labels, had been surprisingly satisfying, she'd thought, as she'd taken a break and prepared lunch, having pegged Tinker, Tailor, Soldier, Spy onto her clotheshorse.

By the middle of the afternoon, Alice had really found her mojo in the hallway. Armfuls of trinkets were swept up, along with a pile of stained and redundant takeaway menus, a chipped lamp, three broken umbrellas and some framed pastel drawings of indeterminable animals and flowers which she'd done and which had faded to a deathly pallor. The two bikes, she'd decided, would have to remain here until she'd bought and erected a shed for them in the back garden. Alice gave them a good clean, stacked them against the wall and stepped back to examine them, almost tripping over RUBBISH and RECYCLE which were bulging with satisfaction.

Now it's Sunday and time for the big one: the sitting room. After breakfast – a loveselfcare-recommended energy-rich green smoothie that tasted and looked like her paintbrush water - she untangles her headphone wires, pushes the white plastic buds into her ears and connects to her phone. The soothing spiritual accompaniment recommended by the tidying gurus will keep her clear-headed when faced with difficult emotional choices.

She hadn't noticed just how crowded the sitting room was until she'd taken time to have a close look last night. Everything is so familiar that it's become almost invisible. The surfaces are covered with holiday souvenirs, things she has liked the look of and picked up on long walks, books, magazines, CDs, paperwork, cat toys, some unfinished knitting - she can't recall what it is that's unfinished - and a growing collection of Welsh pottery.

There is a generous dispersal of spider plants – she loves taking cuttings and repotting them, as they are so easy to look after. An enormous Swiss Cheese plant and an equally prodigious Weeping Fig stand diagonally opposite each other, filling out two corners of the room like heavyweight champions eyeing up their opponents in a boxing ring. And how has she accumulated so much mismatched furniture? Two Victorian sideboards and a glass cabinet, three different chairs, and a large sofa that grapples for space with the coffee table a friend had made from a fallen oak tree. *This isn't going to be straightforward*, she thinks, as she sits in the cat's armchair and pulls at a pair of thermal socks that are stuck down the side of the seat.

Alice puts her faith in the music and her ability to meet the challenge. At first, she quite enjoys the memories triggered by her eclectic treasures. Memories of backpacking as a student when she'd bought small, cheap keepsakes like coasters, magnets and pill boxes, because she could stuff them into her rucksack and because she was broke.

Foreign memorabilia upped its game as she acquired a decent salary and developed her innate good taste. There is a beautiful glazed ceramic water jug from the foothills of the Pyrenees next to the elegant Himalayan singing bowls she had hauled back from Kathmandu, promising herself she would learn how to use them while all this time they've remained silent. Marble wine goblets from Milan, tapestry cushions from Bruges, African woodcarvings, South American pottery. All these and so much more create an aesthetic map of her life, her friends and the things she enjoys doing.

Before she knows it, two hours pass in which she revisits her kaleidoscope of possessions, picking them up, examining them, occasionally laughing at a situation recalled and unexpectedly crying at the recollection of unrequited young love. Two hours and nothing is condemned to the compostable bin bags of shame. She has FULL block. FULL blindness.

Waves of meditative music crash around in Alice's head making her brain feel seasick. She collapses into the ocean of scatter cushions on her sofa, pulls out the earbuds and throws them on the floor. Her queasiness subsides as the gentle murmurs of her home – the soft shudder of the fridge, the hum of her computer, the wind teasing the creaky letterbox - return to soothe her. Clarity, which has also been absent today, now drops in to see if it can offer any help.

Alice remembers that the headphones were a birthday present from her sister, along with a bullet point list of ideas on how she should use them to improve and enrich herself and her life:

- listening to motivational music while out walking or on training runs or when she's getting into the zone for painting
- enjoying audiobooks on the train to work
- watching films, television programmes and downloaded tutorials for her psychology course, anywhere, anytime and without interruption from the noisy distraction of the world at large
- reading improving blogs and listening to life-affirming vlogs

Alice has no idea what a vlog is and doesn't want to find out either. Her sister said she could even watch dating site videos and testimonials – age appropriate of course – and finally find a suitable soulmate.

Staring at her collection of antique glassware in the display cabinet, she ponders the alleged benefits of the lifeless headphones sprawled across the floor. Motivational music and podcasts certainly help her to run faster and walk further but she no longer hears the morning birdsong nor the breeze gossiping in the branches overhead. She listens to books but misses the pattern of words, the texture of pages, the soundscape of passengers and of travel. She may be more cultured, more educated but what's the point of it all if it means she spends most of her time in her own company?

Alice wonders if this is what her sister yearns for. Space and solitude in her busy yet unproductive and inopportune family and working lives. After all, it was her sister who'd also recommended loveselfcare.com. Entirely converted, she claimed the FULL technique had unveiled the purpose in her life, re-ignited her energy, her self-worth. She'd chosen to commit to the infinite path of possibility, optimism, connection, resilience and responsibility. In time, she knew that her family would come to terms with the evangelical purge of their home and her children would start speaking to her again. In fact, they'd probably thank her.

She sits up onto the edge of the sofa, elbows leaning on knees, her head resting in her hands. *I'm just not the same as her*, she thinks. Alice tries and fails to recall the last time she went away with her running and hill-walking groups or to the theatre or a concert with friends. *I've let her and her ideas get in the way*. Looking at Rasputin's chair opposite her, she notes that even he's been avoiding her for some time.

Alice considers the reasons why she has a whole weekend free to embark upon this decluttering fiasco and realises, as she looks for a pen and some paper, that a different kind of action is required.

Within half an hour, she has devised and written her own FULL programme. It is much simpler than what is proposed by loveselfcare.com. Hereafter, it declares, she will only engage in activities that are FUN, UPLIFTING, make her LAUGH or enrich her LIFESTYLE. *How easy was that*? she thinks. *Maybe I should email it to loveselfcare.com and they could embrace it in their unique philosophy.*

The cuckoo clock that Alice had bought while on holiday with friends in Switzerland announces the evening's arrival. She decides it's time to stop listening to her sister. Time to start listening to herself again and to the world beyond herself. Her life was full before those wretched headphones appeared and before loveselfcare.com intervened. Full of friends, full of experiences, full of enjoyment yet to come. Her home may be crowded but it's packed with memories of experiences and of people; everything she owns has a function and a use; each item is loved, even if it is not looked at regularly. She decides that she is not going to let anyone persuade her to throw it all away.

Alice retrieves all the rejects and returns them to their rightful places, uttering words of apology as she does so. By midnight, RUBBISH sits alone on the coffee table. Opening it and looking inside, she notices that most of the contents are gifts from her sister. She takes RUBBISH outside, smiling at the repurposed headphone wires wound around its top and tied in a knot. The earbuds wobble in a final protest as she slams the dustbin lid down and walks back to her life.

Moira Harris

Action and consequence

'There you go, mate.'

The muted rattle of two coins being dropped into the almost empty cardboard coffee cup and colliding with the other small change wakes him. He's never far from consciousness, just like a child who never ventures far from the edge of the pool when learning to swim. It's just too dangerous. You don't know what might happen.

His stiff neck is incapable of lifting his leaden head so he mumbles a thankyou from inside his jacket hood. Exhausted, hungry and numb with cold, he hugs his knees into his chest to try and generate some heat. The concrete wall of the building against which he is sitting grates his spine while his seat – a bin bag stuffed with newspapers – provides a poor barrier against the chill pavement.

A woman walking on the opposite side of the road suddenly stops as though she's encountered an invisible wall. The young man listening to an audiobook as he strides in her wake, hands thrust deep in pockets, eyes staring at the ground, bumps into her. 'For fucks sake, love.' He adjusts his noise-cancelling headphones and continues on his march, dissolving into the anonymity of bodies heading for workplaces. Unaware of him, she cannot move and starts to shiver uncontrollably. A repetitive thud starts up inside her skull, its volume rising in a crescendo to a heavy hammering. *I can't face going into the office yet*. As she turns to walk back to the station, she sees the café next to her. With the little remaining energy that hasn't seeped from her cold, fragile body, she propels herself through the door.

***

Every day his restricted view, framed by his torn hood, is exactly the same. His soulless eyes follow the movement of legs and feet that pass back and forth in front of him. Smart leather shoes, high heels, designer trainers, boots, sandals, all changing in accordance with the changing seasons. All so different from the synthetic newspaper-stuffed loafers he wears.

Beyond this he sees the rectangle of road that lies between him and the café. Cars, taxis, cyclists and red double decker buses fill the space. He used to have a pass that enabled him to ride the warm night buses but he lost it when he was mugged and beaten up. His empty stomach groans but, as usual, he will count a hundred pairs of black, laced shoes, from left to right, before looking in the coffee cup. Sometimes his patience is rewarded.

***

She sits by the large picture window in the café. A thin lace curtain of drizzle creeps down the glass. Her hands rest on the over-sized mug of black coffee. The caffeine is supposed to be restoring order to her head, combatting her hangover. Fragmented images from last night, like the shards of a smashed window, stab at her thoughts. Tears threaten to erupt as she desperately tries to re-assemble her memory. But it's too difficult. Just like her young niece's jigsaw puzzles with their missing pieces.

***

Shit, was that fifty-seven or fifty-eight? He's an expert on losing. He could write a Ph.D. on the subject: how it is possible not to look after the important stuff in life. He'd promised that he would take care of his daughter and that she didn't need anyone else's help. If the authorities got involved, they would take her away. What kind of father would allow that? But what kind of a father couldn't see that his teenage daughter had a gambling addiction?

He tried everything he could think of but she was always one step ahead. Her plausible lies and unthinkable deceits convincingly concealed the severity of her destructive obsession. *It wasn't her doing this to us*, he used to tell himself. It was the illness that caused the cravings for the desired rush and excitement. But by whatever means he rationalised her behaviour, whatever he did to try and help her quit, it was never enough.

In the end he gambled on her by re-mortgaging the house to give her money and fund her counselling. The stakes proved too high and he lost everything as swiftly as she had accumulated thousands of pounds of debt: his job, his marriage, his family, his friends, his home, his identity. He is now the sole companion to his invisible self.

**

Beneath the café's harsh lighting, the ruby at the heart of her engagement ring looks like a drop of blood. She and her girlfriend had exchanged rings on the 29th of February. They'd heard about the tradition of women proposing to men on this date and decided it would be fun to adopt the long-standing custom for their own needs. After living together for two years, they'd recently bought an apartment in a new development at Paddington Quay. *Why the hell did I sleep with someone else last night*? This week her fiancée is away on a lecture tour. Why did I bring her back to our home?

She shivers at the patchwork memory of it all. She had gone to her favourite wine bar after a successful day during which she'd acquired an extremely influential client for her advertising agency. She recalls sharing a lot of laughter and a bottle of Krug champagne bought by an older woman who'd asked if she could join her; long, blonde hair covering her face as they kissed in the taxi; more drinks and a couple of joints at the apartment; being undressed by a stranger; alone this morning, staring at a single diamond earring cradled in a crease in the pillow beside her; rushing to the bathroom to throw up.

**

'Bloody lazy bastard.' Two ugly laughs shatter the cold morning air as the coffee cup is kicked over. His body tenses, waiting to defend itself from what's about to come. This time, though, danger chooses not to stop, not to deliver the punches, kicks and abuse that it revels in whenever it offers itself to him. It was why he'd got rid of the 'HUNGRY AND HOMELESS – PLEASE HELP' message he'd written on a piece of cardboard; it had attracted the wrong sort of attention.

His muscles relax and he collects the scattered coins from the wet pavement. There isn't enough for breakfast. Not even enough for an over-priced cup of tea. *I deserve all of this.*

***

She stares out of the window and straight through the beggar shuffling around on his hands and knees on the opposite pavement. I don't deserve any of this. A cocktail of caffeine and paracetamol begins to work its magic. She knows that she must forget what happened, not let guilt carve its way into her conscience. Surely her behaviour last night was out of character?

She can't apologise for being charming, intelligent and attractive. It is, after all, what makes her so good at her job and supports their lifestyle. A shadow of a smile plays around the corners of her mouth as she thinks again about what happened in the darkness of her bedroom.

'Do you mind if I sit here?' She looks up at the man carrying a coffee and a large chocolate croissant on a tray. His smile awaits her reply. Gathering up her coat and bag, she says she is leaving. The rain has stopped and she fills her lungs with clear, cold air as she crosses the road.

***

He rises up on his knees just as the expensively-dressed woman steps onto the kerb. His light-headedness almost makes him lose his balance but he steadies himself. Her face seems kind, like the face of an angel, and he is hopeful. As she stops to open her leather hand-bag and reach inside, he lifts the cup and closes his eyes. He can taste hot, sweet tea.

'Hi darling. Just phoning to say I love you. Call me.' She puts her phone back in her bag and her knee-high boots are soon lost among the forest of legs. He sits back against the wall and withdraws into his hood.

One, two, three, four….

La dolce vita

The startled pigeons are first to respond to the shouting. They ascend to the rooftops in a flustered formation as Chloe looks up from her book and across the piazza to where the loud voices are coming from. She sees three waiters waving their arms like some kind of crazy semaphore at a man on the terrazza of a busy cafe.

'What d'you think's happening over there?'

Natasha glances up then returns her attention to her phone. 'Probably one of those north Africans trying to sell dodgy sun hats to the tourists. Haven't you noticed they're everywhere?'

The action has erupted very quickly, like a playground fight with the bullies surrounding their victim. People drift across Chloe's line of sight like a curtain in a breeze and she glimpses the man bending, then bobbing up and down. Was he punched just then? She's not sure. The man extracts himself from the commotion, backing away with hands held high in defeat before merging into the crowds. The tall, slim Italian assailants, each one dressed in tailored black shirts and trousers, smooth back their designer haircuts. They briefly exchange masculine looks of superiority then screw their theatrical smiles in place before turning to their customers to offer expansive apologies.

Chloe wonders whether Italy's volcanic geology has been absorbed by the country's occupants across the centuries. She wants to mention this to Natasha but recognises that her friend is not very communicative today. *Perhaps it's the heat and a lack of sleep*, she thinks, as she returns to the Let's Explore guide she's been gripping for the last few minutes. Then Chloe reads a paragraph that she's sure will interest Natasha.

'Isn't this place just amazing, Tash?'

13

'Uh huh.' Natasha scrolls down her Smartphone while pressing an ice-cold bottle of water to her forehead.

'It says that Mel Gibson filmed The Passion of Christ here.'

'Really.'

'Yeah. Apparently, Matera looks exactly like Jerusalem and the Holy Land.'

'Wow.'

Sighing, Chloe shuts her book and puts it next to her empty coffee cup on the wooden table. The voice of Pavarotti singing La donna e mobile hurtles through the open restaurant windows for the second time as the CD continues on its loop. She glances at her watch, wondering if they'll do any more sightseeing now that they've had lunch. *Five more minutes of people watching and then I'll say something*, Chloe decides.

The unfamiliar silence between the two girls and the space it occupies have both expanded during recent days. In the small room they share at Oxford, they stay up late talking, drinking with friends – mostly Natasha's – and working hard on assignments. Chloe often helps Natasha with her essays, sometimes writing large chunks of them. Chloe doesn't mind though. She's a naturally high-achieving academic, which had been tough in her school where many students left at sixteen with few qualifications. Chloe had been anxious about going to Oxford, worried about whether or not she'd fit in. The surprise she'd felt when the well-off, confident and good-looking Natasha had shown an interest in her, was buried beneath the absolute relief of finding a friend.

It was at an end of term cocktails night that the girls had agreed upon a trip to Italy as a well- earned reward for their excellent first year English exam results. Chloe, while losing the battle with her hangover the following day, expressed her concern about funding the holiday. She'd spent her student loan and daren't ask her Mum for more money. Life had been challenging after her parents' divorce ten years ago. Her Dad just disappeared and her Mum juggled three jobs to provide for herself and Chloe. Unsurprisingly, Natasha had the solution to Chloe's financial problem.

'My step-father will easily pay for it,' she said, sitting up in bed and swallowing two paracetamols with strong, black coffee.

'Are you sure, that's OK?' croaked Chloe, from her side of the room.

'Oh yes,' said Natasha, adjusting her pillow. 'Clive will do anything for me if he knows what's good for him.'

The girls had threaded their way down Italy's boot towards its stiletto, venturing far beyond the privileged bubble of college life. They had to make decisions about the kind of matters that were invisibly dealt with at Oxford. Chloe was content with cheap travel and hostel accommodation. Natasha, however, insisted on first-class seats and comfortable hotels.

When the money ran out at the beginning of the third week, Clive transferred some more. Chloe took responsibility for planning their travel itinerary, packing it full of historical and cultural sites. She had never been abroad and was overwhelmed by the depth of beauty and the exquisite tastes of Italy's cities, towns, villages, countryside and its people. Natasha had travelled to many parts of the world on expensive sightseeing holidays with her parents. She had certain expectations as a tourist and didn't share Chloe's depth of curiosity unless there was a decent bar, restaurant, spa or swimming pool in the daily schedule.

The minutes pass and Chloe's voice tiptoes across the table. 'Perhaps we should carry on?'

Natasha, now sitting back in her chair, stares at the hot blue sky and hugs the bottle of water to her sternum. 'I'd rather die than visit another bloody Baroque church.'

Chloe fiddles with her souvenir soft leather bookmark that is trapped between the pages she's been reading. A thin ribbon of sweat uncurls down her spine.

'Crucifixions, breast-feeding Madonnas, Nativities, Last Suppers and, oh my God, so many bloody saints! Couldn't those guys paint anything else?'

'Perhaps you should go back to the hotel, Natasha?'

'And this heat is just too much.'

'Maybe have a lie down and cool off a bit?'

Natasha groans. 'We should just go to the coast if it carries on like this.'

Chloe has no more suggestions. Her attention has shifted to a familiar figure approaching across the shiny, worn cobbles of the piazza.

'Chloe, what do you think? The coast?'

It is the man who had been chased away by the waiters.

'Wouldn't it be lovely to be by the sea in this heat?'

When she doesn't get a reply, Natasha stops her sky-gazing, sits up and sees the man. 'Oh God, Chloe, just ignore him.'

Chloe has never seen such beautiful dark skin. The smooth ebony tones seem highly polished beneath the layer of sweat covering the man's face. His neck is long and slim and his kind eyes keep watch above noble cheekbones. The dusty, ill-fitting brown suit he wears over an old Keep Calm and Carry On T-shirt belongs to another man's shadow. He stops in front of Chloe, his bare head bent, grazed hands clasped before him, feet shifting his light frame from side to side. The broken sole of his right sandal hangs limply beneath his toes.

Chloe quickly scans around for waiters but they've retreated to the cool interior of the restaurant. He lifts his head to glimpse the loose change lying on top of the girls' bill in a small white saucer. Then he looks at Chloe and begins speaking to her. His voice is just louder than a whisper, and his words, although clear, occasionally stumble in his desert-dry throat.

'Please, Signorina, have you some money for food? Soldi per il cibo? I'm trying to – '

'No, we don't,' says Natasha, closing her eyes behind her sunglasses and reclining again in her chair.

'Tasha?' Chloe wishes her friend had gone back to the hotel.

Natasha sits upright and slams the water bottle onto the table in final judgement. Chloe jumps but the man doesn't move.

'God's blessings upon you both,' he says, then turns and walks away.

'We should have given him something.'

Natasha holds her defiant pose. 'What for? So that he can drink my money away?'

'Your money?'

Chloe holds her breath, considering what to do next. Then she grabs her bag and runs after the man. Her tense muscles anticipate Natasha's grip on her arm but nothing holds her back.

'Wait,' she says as she reaches him. 'Where are you from?' The man stops. Several seconds amble by as his shoulders relax back and down and he appears to grow taller. Then he turns around. Chloe is startled by the intensity of his proud, direct stare. She can't help but look into the deep coal-black holes of his eyes from where his anguish is mined.

'Northern Nigeria, Miss.' The voice is stronger than before.

'So why are you here?'

His face fights to remain expressionless.

'I am a Christian, Miss. Nigeria is too dangerous for me. Extremists burned my village, murdered my wife, our new-born baby.' He closes his eyes. Afternoon church bells sing across the town and out into the surrounding fields.

'I'm so sorry.' Chloe is embarrassed to hear her pathetic, feeble voice. She senses the words mocking her as they run off like children into the hot summer air.

The man opens his eyes and finds some more words. 'I escaped here with my mother and my other children. I am a teacher but cannot find work. I will do anything. But I can only ask strangers for charity.'

Chloe has some understanding of the difficulties faced by those perceived as outsiders. She's read the hate-fueled graffiti on the metal shutters of shops in her High Street, seen windows smashed on her estate, fights, abuse, intimidation. An untraceable force drives the fear on, urging it to circulate like an angry rush of Chinese Whispers.

The man tilts his head as though someone standing behind his right shoulder is talking to him. Chloe recognises the exhaustion of someone striving for the hour by hour, day to day survival of his family. She is reminded of a wild animal that has no concept of its future and is fleeing from its pursuer.

'Please have this.' Chloe pushes a folded note into the man's right hand and closes his fingers over it.

He examines his balled fist as though he doesn't recognize it. A fragile smile gathers across his cracked lips and he swallows his sorrow.

'Thank you for your kindness and generosity, Miss. And for talking to me. May God bless you and may he bless your family. All of Heaven's Blessings be upon you.'

She can't think of anything to say. No one's ever blessed her. Chloe nods and steps backwards. The man's smile is one of immense gratitude but she cannot bear to look at his joyless eyes. She ends the encounter by slowly retracing her path back to Natasha. She resists the urge to see if the man is still watching her until she arrives at the cafe. Then Chloe looks back but he is gone.

'I think the heat must be getting to you, Clo-Clo.' Natasha is putting sun cream on her lightly tanned arms.

Chloe picks up her book, weighing it in her hands.

'Well, did you give him anything?'

Chloe flicks through the pages. 'Twenty euros.'

'Twenty? To a beggar? Christ, Chloe, that's four cocktails at Happy Hour.'

Pavarotti's voice has been replaced by Callas singing Oh mio babbino caro. 'I'd like to go now,' says Chloe.

Natasha applies some lip gloss, her eyes unreadable behind Jackie O sunglasses.

Chloe breathes deeply and looks at the day's itinerary clipped to the inside cover of the travel guide. 'There are still some places we should visit, you know.'

Natasha stands up, adjusting her hat and her sundress.

'And we really should go to the Cathedral again. It was so crowded earlier.'

'Do whatever you want,' says Natasha, picking up her shoulder bag. 'I'm going back to the hotel.'

Chloe watches her friend stride off like a catwalk model, heads turning as the tall figure cuts through the crowds. Natasha has never spoken to her like this before and she's not sure what to do. Confrontation is something that Chloe prefers to avoid. She puts her book in her bag and lets her intuition take her for a walk.

Chloe spends the rest of the hot afternoon wandering in and out of the maze of shaded lanes that serpentine through the old city. Siesta time disperses the crowds and she bathes in its gentle calm. She also realises how much more she appreciates her surroundings without Natasha's whining voice as an accompaniment. No complaints about the places they're visiting, no grumbles about sore feet, an aching back, the heat, when they'll eat, where the next coffee is. What did Natasha expect?

Both girls had been so excited when they arrived in Matera by train yesterday morning. Natasha was looking forward to a swim and a full body massage in the converted monastery which was their luxury spa hotel. Chloe was eager to discover the extraordinary heritage of the old city. Unable to get into their hotel room until two o'clock, they' left their luggage at reception and began exploring the city. According to the film they watched in the history museum, the city is one of the oldest in Europe, having been inhabited for 7000 years. Natural limestone caves were the first dwellings until others were carved from the gentle rock and then built upon. Over centuries the town expanded and later declined and was forgotten until its malaria-ridden occupants were re-housed in the 1950s.

A battle was fought and won to save Matera and its rich history from the total decay the authorities wished for. Tears escaped from the corners of Chloe's eyes as she watched the slow demise and later the restoration of both the city and its inhabitants. Touching the caramel-cream stone buildings, Chloe was absorbed into its warmth and heritage and she sensed the spirits of successive generations. Natasha, however, had acquired the tourist demeanour of plodding feet and rounded shoulders as she peered into what she could only regard as the gloomy cave spaces of homes, churches, art galleries and museums.

Chloe rests beneath a long-neglected olive tree, the arthritic twists of its branches like swollen knuckles. The tree is one of several in what was once a thriving olive grove. The silvery green leaves would have shimmered softly throughout the summer until the harvest brought laughing parties of pickers with their hampers and rugs in readiness for feasts and celebrations.

The olive grove is now a park and the ancient companions, their arbours barren, watch over young mothers playing with their children, elderly gentlemen squabbling as they cheat at cards, and secret lovers' trysts. Today the trees listen to Chloe's thoughts and sympathise with her dilemma.

She reflects on how Natasha's behaviour towards her in Italy has gradually revealed itself to be very different from how she treats her at university. They had embarked on this trip as good friends - or so she thought - but now, more often than not, they seem to get on each other's nerves. Chloe wonders whether she and Natasha would benefit from a few days apart before continuing with their adventure. Natasha could go to the beach while she remained here in Matera. But she can't rely on the generosity of her friend's stepfather for much longer. As she watches two little naked girls playing in a fountain, Chloe considers that it might be time for her to return home and find a summer job.

Her phone pings just at that moment when she's not sure which side of sleep she is on. Chloe reads the text and groans. She hugs her knees towards her chest and rests her forehead on them. The old olive tree leans over her, curious to know why she is so disturbed.

C U at Art Cafe in Via Bruno at 6. Massimo and Roberto meeting us. Best aperitivi in town! Nx

Last night they had shared a table with the two boys at a gelateria. Natasha had talked while Chloe watched the young Italians fix their perfect white-toothed smiles on the attractive blonde, their black eyes sweeping across her like searchlights. Chloe had enjoyed her ice cream as she watched her friend tease and tempt her prey. She didn't say much, even though her Italian was much better than Natasha's. Nor had she cared that neither of the boys had flirted with her. Chloe knew that her short, square figure and her frizzy brown hair were no competition for Natasha. As the girls stood to leave, Chloe saw the Italians gazing at Natasha and was reminded of two happy, trusting puppies waiting to be drowned.

Before meeting Natasha, Chloe visits the cathedral again, pleased to find it's almost empty. There is space for her to appreciate the surrounding craftsmanship: the fresco of the Last Judgement with the sword-wielding Archangel Michael running among the sinners; the side chapel containing a fifteenth century intricately carved crib scene incorporating features of Matera into the rural biblical landscape.

People are lighting small candles in front of a statue in the nave. Chloe stands away from the group, admiring the calm expression on the dark-skinned face of the Madonna della Bruna. She is Matera's patron saint who guards the city and who is still worshipped by its inhabitants. Chloe has seen so many representations of Madonnas since arriving in Italy but nothing like this one. She has a sudden sense of loss, of loneliness. Her eyes sting and the saint becomes a blur.

Church bells announce six o'clock as Chloe arrives at the top of the busy Via Bruno. The cooling evening has encouraged tourists and locals into the city's busy street. Chloe stands and looks up at the beautiful old buildings which provide the backdrop to cafés, restaurants, art galleries and shops. She no longer feels alone as she walks among people's laughter and chatter and looks for the Art Café.

Chloe just finishes rehearsing her speech to Natasha when the explosion rips through the air. Instinct forces her to the ground and

20

makes her cover her head with her hands, squeezes her eyes shut. Time has fled and Chloe has no idea how long she remains huddled on the pavement. Looking up, she watches the silent horror film before her. Except it's not a film.

She struggles to her feet, uninjured, but covered in the white dust of centuries. It forms clouds in front of her, from which people emerge like ghosts, running, staggering, their mouths open but their screams muted. She moves against the tide of terrified victims, searching for the Art Cafe among the shattered buildings.

'Tasha! Tasha!'

A woman with long hair is rocking and sobbing on a plastic chair, clutching a bundle to her chest. It's not Natasha.

Chloe trips and nearly falls over a twisted leg protruding from beneath a crumpled parasol. A broken sandal hangs off the foot. She crouches to push the parasol away and finds the Nigerian teacher. His eyes are like wide open windows and his lips move, repeatedly making the same shapes. Chloe still cannot hear anything except the thunder of her blood as though her head is under water.

The man shivers and clutches the side of his body with his left hand. His blood hides the words Carry On as it is spreads across his T-shirt. She holds his other hand and bends her head to his, feeling his breath against her ear. Eventually two words emerge. 'Bless you.'

'You're going to be OK. Just hold on. Please stay with me.' She hears the words form in her head but they seem distant as they leave her mouth. Chloe tries to make him comfortable, placing her bag under his head and covering his chest with a ripped tablecloth. She strokes his face until his rasping breath ceases and his body is motionless. Chloe removes her hand from his cooling grip as her grief arrives to rampage through her body. Anger isn't far behind, watching and waiting as her tears slip down from her cheeks and mix with the crumpled and bloodied twenty-euro note that sits in her open palm.

Moira Harris

The art of life

Stella shifts her numb bottom from one side of the hard metal seat to the other. Cold penetrates her thin, black polyester skirt and begins a slow crawl up and down through her bones. The snagged charcoal grey tights retrieved from the bedroom floor in the early morning's darkness now pucker around her ankles in cheap nylon air pockets.

Stella's cushioned leather chair had disappeared from the corner of Room 7 over the weekend, probably pinched by the pushy redhead from Visiting Exhibitions. She'd been unable to confront the irritating young woman before her shift started because the temporary traffic lights in the High Street had made Stella late again. Stella decides to go to Visiting Exhibitions during her lunch hour and alleviate her discomfort.

She wriggles her icy toes inside the mandatory wide-fitting lace-ups and watches her feet trace the thin, dark lines on the polished parquet floor. The honey-coloured wooden blocks form geometric patterns of arrows that point to nowhere. Stella often tries to count them but a member of the public or staff will usually interrupt with a question about toilets or rotas. Before answering, Stella endeavours to imprint upon her memory an aspect of the block she has reached; an idiosyncrasy of the pattern, a scuff or indentation. But the situation is hopeless because the pieces of this huge jigsaw are so alike. Stella has no choice but to start the count again in the hope of overtaking her current tally of 2,347. There was a time when she'd employed a piece of fluffy Blue Tac found in one of her pockets to act as a marker. She'd walk across the room while appearing to consider the question just posed, bend down as if to pick something from the floor and stick the Blue

23

Tac in place. A fantastic idea until the marker disappeared out into the street on the sole of someone's shoe.

Tuesday morning in March and as usual, the Civic Art Museum welcomes a trickle of visitors. Rain that splattered across her bus window in huge diagonal tears has followed Stella indoors. Now it dribbles puddles from umbrellas or re-forms itself in diminishing footprint paths. The cleaners on the evening shift will be busy.

Stella is always relieved to be back at work after her day off but who wouldn't be, given her choices. Watching time stagnate in the gallery is preferable to the suffocating atmosphere of her home. Her left hand has its own agenda as it searches for the badge on her lapel jacket. Stella can't recall seeing it in her reflection in the mirror above the bathroom sink earlier this morning. But the badge is still attached so there can be no mistaking who she is. Her pale, bony fingers wander further up to find some loose strands of hair escaping from her pony tail. Stella draws them down in front of her eyes, examining the split ends before tucking them behind her left ear where they are soon forgotten.

A complaining stomach reminds her to buy some breakfast cereal on the way home tonight. Not that she's bothered by empty kitchen cupboards in the morning. Stella is a strong coffee person in the early hours. Two heaped teaspoons in a mug, add hot water and after a few sips, she's in the world again. Today, however, she is really hungry, having eaten so little yesterday.

Stella gets up and walks the length of the room engaging her heel to toe method. Her snail's pace record for covering twenty metres is an impressive five and a half minutes. She adopts a more authoritative stance, occupying her full height, when a young couple enter the room. They look like art students from the local university, probably more interested in dodging the weather than in viewing the paintings.

The girl advances with the confidence of a catwalk model in thigh-high red and black-striped socks, the tops of her slim, bare legs disappearing into miniscule denim shorts. Removing her corduroy cap, a wave of thick, shiny hair pours like rich, dark chocolate down the back of her soft leather jacket. The tall, curly-haired young man draws her into the warmth of his three-quarter length woollen coat. He kisses her smooth, tanned forehead and she laughs as his strong, unshaven chin tickles her nose.

They sidle around the room, often pausing to whisper a few words or exchange a gentle caress. For a brief moment the girl's eyes are held in Stella's gaze and Stella recognises the fire that will later consume the young man. It nudges at her like a faded memory buried beneath years of disappointment; a creased black and white photo pulled from behind the sofa cushions revealing another time of youthful embarrassment, an awakening of passion, desire, hope.

In her teens, Stella was desperate to go to art college but pregnancy, then marriage to Alan and the swift arrival of two more children dumped her dreams in storage forever. After years of mundane employment in the service industry she was so excited to get the job in the museum. How ridiculous, she'd often thought, pretending to equate her services with those of the law, finance and pharmaceuticals. Oh yes, she'd been most industrious as a cleaner and carer but the pay was small compensation, and her current job is a poor attempt to make up for a momentary misjudgement and its consequences. After five years of staring at the exhibits in Room 7, Stella could probably reproduce each one of them given the chance.

The twelve contemporary paintings, a mixture of landscape and portrait, are the early works of an artist who later won international fame as a sculptor. They hang in forgotten exile beneath halos of dusty artificial light in this, the artist's home town museum. If she closes her eyes Stella can see the marks and brushstrokes of each composition painted on identically sized canvases, five feet by three feet. The muted colours of local countryside scenes perfectly match those of the dirty washing up water she gazes into every evening, while a kaleidoscope of heavily applied oils portrays confused faces. Strange animal figures stand and sit in fields. What possessed him to attempt painting horses is something she'll never comprehend. Everyone knows the challenges and pitfalls of equine art can only be met and avoided after years of practice.

The radical shift in composition of the twelfth picture sets it apart from its compatriots and marks the significant turning point in the artist's journey. Stella watches the young couple stop to examine it. Two subjects: in the foreground, a dark-suited man holding a letter in one hand and a small suitcase in the other. His tear-filled eyes stare straight into the gallery space; in the mid-ground, a golden-haired woman wearing a long red dress, her back turned towards the young man and her face hidden; in front of her is a dense forest, forming the background. *Departure.* A highly charged emotional radiance in bold brushstrokes that makes visitors linger. The young observers say nothing as they stand in front of the painting for several long minutes. Then they fold further into each other and leave the room.

Once she'd settled into the job, Stella had expressed her surprise to the Curator, Mr Jackman, that none of the visitors wanted to discuss the pictures with her.

'You're not employed to educate people, Stella. You're here to make sure they don't nick anything, OK?'

There is the occasional exchange concerning the location of toilets, café, museum shop and exits as well as opening and closing times. She dreads confrontation with members of the public and having to discourage people from taking photographs, touching the pictures, talking too loudly, allowing their children to run around, eating and drinking in the building. A dismissive grunt or a derogatory reference to her appearance or character are the usual responses.

She's been instructed not to smile or stare at visitors too much because it makes them feel uncomfortable. According to Mr. Jackman, all museum and art gallery wardens across the entire planet are considered a necessary evil. Stella hates the title of warden and its associations with traffic offences and the prison service. She'd tried smiling but people looked straight through her or spoke to her as if she was an idiot. She gave up and instead cultivated a thick skin like the layers of paint on the Old Masters she admires downstairs. No one is interested in Stella's views on art. No one, it seems, is interested in her views on anything.

Last week Stella was reprimanded by Mr Jackman for arguing with an arrogant art expert. She thought they'd had a robust exchange of views about the shortcomings of the horses and had enjoyed the discussion. How could she have known that the woman was a descendant of the artist? Stella had apologised to Mr Jackman while silently cursing the complainant. She couldn't afford to lose the little security and the bubbles of freedom that the warden's position provides.

She took the job when Alan lost his, and for five years she has watched her husband's pride and anger slowly devour him.

Nobody is interested in an unreliable fifty-something welder, so he is settled into a routine of unemployment which he performs from the comfortable depths of his television armchair. At least the children have done well, recognising their escape route via hard work at school and university. Stella had encouraged them and now they live their own sophisticated lives far from the provincial backwater they grew up in.

The morning drags on. A dozen people walk through the room including Lester, who slips in every Tuesday morning after his weekly shower at the leisure centre. He is a thin scrap of a man in his early sixties, his bald head poking out, tortoise-like, from the collar of a duffel coat that is several sizes too large.

'Morning, Lester.'

Lester says nothing but nods to Stella, as he always does.

Once a successful lawyer, he'd apparently suffered a breakdown many years ago following a very difficult court case. He lost the power of speech along with everything else he possessed, including his wife and children. Lester is a familiar character in the town, accepting the smallest degree of charity but never a bed nor any other form of refuge. As usual, he stops to consider each painting, his arthritic fingers intertwined behind his back like a hidden game of here's the church, here's the steeple.

Stella wonders whether Lester is suffering from some kind of memory loss as he always views the pictures as though for the first time. He has a repertoire of expressive body movements which Stella can only observe from behind: a vigorous nod or shake of the head, a few steps forwards, backwards or sideways, disentangling his fingers to adopt a hands-on-hips or folded arms pose. He always strides past the final picture, his face turned towards the passageway that leads into the next room. For a brief moment, *Departure* is reflected in the remarkable sheen of his highly polished shoes and then he vanishes for another week.

When the room is empty again, Stella stands, stretches her arms above her head and then bends over to touch her toes. She repeats this ten times before launching into a series of torso side twists, swinging her arms from left to right. Her methods of dealing with boredom also distract her mind from wandering to thoughts of being at home. Without them, she'll begin to wonder what fragment of her husband got out of bed after she went to work; the depressive, the drunk, the irate, the violent, the remorseful.

Today, her thoughts are in the room and she has decided not to look at her watch until she has recited all the books of The Old Testament while jogging on the spot. It is one of the few accomplishments she has salvaged from her childhood in the Girls' Brigade. Jogging is a recent addition. She falters at Lamentations when a sharp twinge stabs at her lower back. She stops to check the time only to discover it too has slowed from a sprint to a leisurely stroll.

Just as Stella is about to sit down again, she notices a distinguished looking elderly gentleman enter the room. His raincoat is draped over his left arm and a smart trilby, held in his right hand, rests against the waistcoat of his well-cut suit. While he examines the summarising paragraphs on the wall next to the paintings, Stella quickly buttons up her jacket and uses an old tissue in her pocket to wipe away the dampness above her top lip and on her forehead. She hopes he didn't hear her gasps from Room 6. Perhaps he's too polite to mention anything. She coughs. He turns around, his smile betraying nothing but generosity. The old man's voice is gentle and kind.

'Good morning, madam. Such dreadful weather we're having.'

'Er, hello, yes, isn't it awful?' Stella remembers her mother calling her madam – a right little madam – when she was naughty as a child.

'My eyesight's not very good in this light,' says the man. Would you mind telling me something about these works please?'

Astonished, Stella forgets about her painful back and delights in sharing her abundant knowledge with him for the next fifteen minutes. They stroll from one painting to the next, the articulate warden pointing out key features as she speaks. He nods, pale blue eyes switching between her and the exhibits, mouth still smiling softly.

'Thank you so much,' he says. I must confess that I've never had the patience for information boards.'

Stella smiles. 'Oh, I can understand that.'

'But my eyesight is genuinely awful in artificial light,' says the man, not wanting Stella to think he's lazy or has taken advantage of her good nature.

'Well, I'm glad to have been of some use, she says,' hoping to conceal her exhilaration.

He offers her a grateful nod and turns to look more closely at Departure. The elated warden's gaze follows the grey-haired visitor across the room. Such a lovely man and so appreciative, she thinks, as he stands with his back to her, unlocking the story on the canvas.

Stella checks her watch again. Nearly lunchtime and she is going to treat herself to something special. Her struggle to choose between a ham and cheese panini and a chicken salad wrap is interrupted by a few gentle sobs. She follows the sound to the man whose head is bent forward over his shuddering body. Stella doesn't know whether to ignore him or to say something. She doesn't want to embarrass him but she is also worried he might be unwell.

'Sir, can I help you at all?'

She sees his arm move towards what must be the neatly folded white handkerchief in his breast pocket. He blows his nose, pushes back his shoulders, raises his head and turns to face Stella.

'I'm dreadfully sorry,' he says. 'Please excuse me, won't you?'

Two pairs of tearful eyes, art and life, young and old, were now looking at her.

'How about a cup of tea, sir?' She's relieved to see that he isn't ill. 'My name's Stella, by the way. What's yours?'

'I'm Richard but you really don't – '

But Stella insists that she really does want to and anyway, it's time for her break. She puts out a call for her lunchtime replacement to take over, then, taking Richard's hat and coat, she guides the elderly visitor towards a table by the window in the empty café. The rain has given up for the day and now the sun shines on the plastic-coated menu standing to attention in its little wooden holder. The small pot of dwarf daffodils, replicated on all the tables, welcomes the rejuvenating light.

Stella is relieved to see the reviving effect of the sweet tea and biscuits as the colour returns to Richard's cheeks. After several more apologies, he tries to explain what has happened.

'Elizabeth and I were married for fifty-three years. She loved art and music, two subjects I was quite ignorant of when we first met.'

Stella remains silent as Richard takes another sip of tea.

Then, straightening himself in his seat, he looks directly into her eyes.

'She taught me so much. When we knew she was dying, she told me quite forcefully not to mope about but to make the most of my life. So that's what I'm doing, travelling the country and visiting museums, attending concerts, going to the theatre.'

'But something else seems to have upset you today,' says Stella in a tone she has practiced much at home.

Richard brushes away some imaginary crumbs on his place mat. 'Today is the anniversary of Elizabeth's death. That beautiful painting brought back the painful memories of her final hours.'

He presses his thin lips together and turns to stare through the window. The little museum courtyard is radiant with the fresh colours of spring. Richard continues, his eyes fixing upon the delicate displays in the flowerbeds.

'We met as young medics, a tough career for a woman back then. But that didn't stop Elizabeth. She had time and energy for her work, her children and all her interests. I was just so lucky to share my life with her.'

Stella places her hand on his forearm. The soft material of his jacket feels expensive beneath her fingers. 'You must miss her very much,' she says.

'Oh, I do,' says Richard, still looking through the glass. 'And I was so angry after she died. Being a doctor doesn't make it any easier.'

Stella pours both of them some more tea. 'Departure is a very powerful work,' she says, trying to redirect his thoughts onto a different path. 'I never tire of looking at it.'

Richard suddenly turns to face her. 'Enough about me,' he says. 'Tell me about yourself, Stella. You're obviously passionate about art.'

She can't remember anyone asking her this question and she almost chokes on her custard cream. Stella offers an edited description of her life and family.

'And that's pretty much me in a tiny nutshell,' she says, running out of words before Richard finishes his tea.

They sit in silence for a while, two strangers considering their contrasting realities. Stella looks at the café clock and tells Richard she must return to work. He stands to gather up his belongings.

'I'm keeping you back, Stella.'

'Not at all,' she says.' It was very good to meet you.'

'Thank you for listening to the ramblings of this sentimental old man.'

When they reach the door of the museum, Richard shakes Stella's hand and holds it as he speaks.

'You have a burning passion for art, my dear. Make sure you don't let that fire go out.'

Stella returns to Room 7 and passes the afternoon in quiet contemplation. A few more visitors file through but she is as unaware of them as they are of her. She's lost the appetite for the lunchtime treat she was supposed to have, and she's forgotten about reclaiming her chair. Stella disappears into her inner world as Richard's departing words spin around and around in her head.

Before she leaves that evening, Stella stands in front of *Departure*. She is always drawn towards the deep, sad eyes of the young man, captured in paint on the verge of leaving. Now, she looks more closely at the woman in the red dress. Stella has always assumed that the artist hid the woman's face as a powerful statement of how she is cruelly rejecting her lover.

She walks closer, resisting the temptation to press her nose against the brushstrokes. A gasp suddenly escapes from her throat as she sees something she has never noticed before on the canvas. It is the faint trace of a narrow pathway snaking through the forest towards the vanishing point. The woman in red is also on a journey. *I've been wrong all this time*, she thinks.

Stella ambles along the pavement in the dying light, smiling at the recollection of her artistic detective work. She approaches her bus stop and images of home crush the memory. Alan was drunk last night and would no doubt repeat the performance tonight. She will tidy around him, give him his tea, put on some washing, listen to the misery of his day, his life and then go to bed. What can her husband teach her? He shares nothing, offers neither love nor affection, just his own self-pity.

Stella passes the university buildings every day. Today she stops to read the notice about evening classes. Her bus goes by as she runs up the steps to the reception office. Pausing before the glass entrance door, she looks at the reflection of her past and her future. Stella pushes open the door and goes inside.

Moira Harris

The waiting is almost over

He crushes the empty cardboard box, smashing and grinding it into the cracked linoleum with the worn heel of his right shoe.

'Evil. Bloody. Bastard.'

He spits the words out, repeating them like a mantra, knowing his voice can't be heard in the bedroom next door. The contents of the box litter the kitchen table and cascade over chairs and onto the floor; dozens of unopened letters scattered about like the fragments of his shattered heart. The same name and address are neatly printed in his handwriting on each identical blue airmail envelope.

He leans forward to press his sweaty palms on the table and stop himself from collapsing onto the battered cardboard beneath his feet. His legs continue to shake uncontrollably as an attack of violent spasms shoots through his body from abdomen to throat. Years of suppressed sorrow, loss and abandonment pour down his crumpled face and soak into the mess on the floor. Gasping for breath, he pulls at his collar and tie to find relief from his suffocating disgust.

'He wanted you to have this after his death.'

The words his aunt had spoken earlier that morning now take another ride on the dodgem cars inside his head. When she'd opened the door to her nephew yesterday, she hadn't recognised him, nor had he known her. He'd arrived three days too late for the funeral but that hadn't bothered him. He may never have returned if his aunt hadn't looked inside the cardboard box.

She'd told him she'd found his address by opening one of the many letters her sister had never received.

'You should know the truth before it's too late,' she'd said, as she'd given him the box that morning.

He'd thanked her, noticing her eyelids fluttering like camera shutters, as they fought to contain her tears. He'd watched her hurry away down the garden path and through the gap where there'd once been a gate, realising how much she reminded him of his mother.

When he decided to return home after such a long time, he wasn't sure what he and his mother would talk about, nor where they would start. But all this concern was extinguished by the shock of finding her bedridden and incapable of speaking due to her most recent stroke. Even during the brief periods when she was awake, she didn't recognise anyone or anything. Having been presented with his correspondence that had been hidden from his mother for so many years, he is now desperate to talk to her. He has so much to say, yet he recognises that the opportunity has passed and that time will soon walk out on them.

The rush of angry emotion and despair has left him exhausted and empty. *I need a drink*, he thinks. He opens the cupboard doors of the large oak Welsh dresser and searches among the random collection of mugs, chipped glasses and plates, packets of sweets and biscuits, balls of wool, offcuts of material, old books and mould-speckled magazines.

At the back he finds an unopened half bottle of brandy. As he removes the bottle his wristwatch knocks against something metal. Instinct tells him to reach inside again and find the object. Feeling the shape and size of it beneath his fingers he soon knows what it is. Rescued from the dark recesses of the cupboard, it doesn't look particularly special as it sits on the Formica table. But there it is, the old, round cake tin in which his mother stores buttons, press studs, toggles, ribbons, bows, zips, patches and anything else she might find useful in her work as a seamstress.

He wipes away the thick layer of dust on the lid to reveal the familiar still life of roses, lilies and greenery. The picture is a copy of an oil painting but the rich reds, yellows, creams and greens of petals and leaves have faded in the shadows of time. The lid is covered with tiny scratches, and small, random patterns of rust peep through the foliage. Flowing garlands of flamingo-pink rosebuds entwined around the tin are interrupted by a few large dents and many more scratches.

He drinks the cheap brandy straight from the bottle while staring at the tin. The sharp liquid claws at his throat but the alcohol temporarily dilutes his anxiety and discomfort. He slumps in a chair and picks up the heavy cake tin and shakes it. A percussive rattling fills the kitchen and his smile is one of recognition. He prises off the rusted lid and buries his fingers into the treasure of his childhood.

'Go and get my buttons and bits box, luvvie,' was what she would ask him when she was working.

Back then, it was just him and his mother sitting in the cosy warmth of the kitchen. He'd been six months old when his father had been killed in a road accident so they had never got to know each other. But there was scant time for his mother to grieve. She needed to employ her sewing skills to provide for both of them.

He'd loved the box's contents. So many different types of buttons, from ones like baby pearls to others almost as large as digestive biscuits. So many textures too: wood, glass, plastic, metal, leather, wool, silk. One day the box contained a hoard of precious jewels, the next a pirate's bounty of silver pieces, then perhaps a vast mine of golden nuggets. The rainbow richness of the buttons pouring through his little fingers onto the kitchen table had fuelled his imagination for hours. Meanwhile, his mother worked at the sewing machine or patiently stitched by hand, often humming along to the music on the radio.

The happiness began to unravel when the iron rule of his step-father invaded their lives. The initial displays of love, tenderness and care were skilled performances to wheedle his way into a struggling mother's heart. But once he crossed that threshold, manipulation was this husband's weapon of control. He started to unpick his wife with words.

'This place is a dump.'

'I'm sorry. I...'

'And this food is disgusting.'

'I'm doing my best but...'

'Well, it just isn't good enough!'

But when the words ceased, the beatings began. The boy would take the box from the cupboard and lose himself in his button world. The radio helped to block out the horror in the room next door.

On one of these occasions his step-father thundered into the kitchen with a handful of wedding photos he'd found in the boy's bedroom. They were the only images he and his mother possessed of his real father. He saw the hatred in the red-blue marbled face of the man and heard the anger as he spoke. 'I'm your father and don't you forget it, you ungrateful little bastard.'

He tried to stop the surge of tears as he watched those rough, brutal hands rip apart the black and white photographs and throw the pieces at his feet. When he knelt to pick them up a hailstorm of buttons fell on top of him as his step-father overturned the table then started to remove the thick leather belt from his waist.

'Maybe this will help you to remember,' he said, as he grabbed the boy by the collar and raised the belt above his head.

The buttons and bits box lost its magic as the years passed by. His mother was always so busy with her work and with trying to avoid confrontation that she had little time to devote to him. At night, his childhood slipped away, bit by bit, and drowned in his tear-soaked pillow. It was replaced by the spirit of a frustrated and sullen young man who was furious with his mother for tolerating so much cruelty. During the day, he learned the wisdom of silence. Consequently, he survived his teenage years without further suffering the physical wrath of his step-father. But he never stopped despising the man.

He left home the day after his step-father tried, for the first and last time, to pick a fight with him. The young man had intervened in the tirade of abuse that was being thrown at his mother about Sunday lunch.

'Don't say another word to her, you bloody pig!'

The entire room rattled as the older man slammed his cutlery on the table and shot up from his chair. 'I'll say what I fucking well want to in my own house!'

The young man was on his feet now. 'It's not your house. It's hers.' He pointed a shaking finger towards his silent mother as she stared down at her untouched food.

'Is that right, Mummy's boy?'

By now, the two men were standing chest to chest in the middle of the floor. The husband clenched his fists, trying to assess his opponent's strength with his wildfire eyes. The son stood tall in terrified defiance, tasting his step-father's stale beer breath while glaring at the repulsive face of his very own Goliath. His mother eventually managed to separate them but knew that tragedy was inevitable if she didn't do something soon.

The following day, after her husband had gone out, she packed a suitcase for her son, gave him all the money she had secretly saved from her sewing and told him to go.

'I can't leave you here with him, Mum.'

But she was insistent, pushing him towards the door before she relented.

'Come with me!' he cried as he stumbled over the doorstep.

'Not now. Later. I promise.'

'Please, Mum, you...'

'For everyone's sake, just go!'

She kissed him, then shut and locked the door on the morning sunshine. She collapsed onto the hallway floor, drawing her body inwards as though it might just vanish and she wouldn't have to bear the sound of his beautiful voice any longer. Her silent scream echoed in her heart and she released her pain into the worn carpet. Outside, the bewildered young man shouted and banged on the door until his broken will fled from him. Drained and defeated, he slowly walked away from the one person he loved and towards an undefined future.

The empty brandy bottle drops from his grip and he wakes up. He's been drifting in and out of the same dream, the one that had brought him home. The one in which he's a child again and where his smiling mother is calling him in from the garden, her open arms waiting to embrace him.

He rubs his eyes and looks down at the unopened letters which are now of no consequence. Turning to the buttons, he sorts them into piles according to type, size and colour. He uses his palette to create faces, animals, flowers - just as he had done as a child. Then, as he moves the cake tin lid to create more space on the table, he recognises something taped to the lid's inner surface.

'Oh my god, Mum. I can't believe you kept it.'

He peels away the yellowing tape to reveal an envelope containing a thin piece of paper that has been read and folded many times. It feels so fragile against the rough skin of his nicotine-stained fingers He knows the contents of the letter by heart and recalls struggling to find the reassuring words he'd written in the hostel. Tucked in next to it is more treasure: an old black and white wedding photo. The discoloured tape that holds its torn pieces together barely hides the jealous destruction it had endured so many years ago.

He goes into the adjacent room and sits in the armchair beside the bed. His mother's fragile breathing gently perforates the silence. She is a diminished figure lost beneath the richly embroidered eiderdown she had lovingly made as a young bride. Her grey face is threaded with age and anguish. Thin, white wisps of hair lie damp against her temples and on the pillow. But he only sees the beautiful angel who, like him, has waited for an answer for so many years.

He places the letter and photo in her small palm and covers them with his hands. As he bows to rest his forehead on the bed, he doesn't see the flicker of her smile before it is extinguished in the evening's fading light.

Happenstance

30 mins L8 cu soon x

She looks at the time on her phone, deletes the text and touches the airplane mode icon. She has no desire to develop a conversation from these scant words. The watery reflection of the screen's blue light floating in the darkness of the restaurant window beside her vanishes as she puts her phone in her bag. She dislikes these abbreviations he's recently introduced. They are so uncharacteristic of a man who is always punctilious about language.

She remembers laughing at his ridiculous use of the emojis, hearts and silly little champagne bottles that she'd found decorating some of his communications as she scrolled through his text messages a few months ago. The laughter had faded to silent disbelief and then anger by the time she'd read the last one, confirming that a bright yellow thumbs down would best illustrate her life.

It's quite late and most people are hurrying through dark, wet city streets, fleeing by bus, train or taxi, into the welcoming depths of homes and families and lovers. She watches a young man and woman, both expensively dressed in fashionable city attire, sitting close to each other in a softly-lit corner of the restaurant. They drink coffee and digestifs, while his forefinger traces shapes across the back of her hand. As he speaks, his lips almost touch her hot cheek. Their gentle laughter dances teasingly around the melancholic notes of the saxophone solo drifting out of the sound system.

Her thoughts are interrupted by the wine waiter serving her a glass of champagne with a flourish and a smile. She explains why the chair opposite her is currently unoccupied but he interrupts with a cascade of reassurances before leaving her to enjoy her aperitif. The first mouthful shoots a message to her brain that she can relax. As the bubbles tap dance on her tongue, she knows that she is in control of all that will happen tonight.

She's had a long day in court, dealing with some challenging cases so this half hour of breathing space, considering the circumstances, is unusually welcome. Space in this almost empty restaurant in which to consider the past and how it will determine her future. She watches the waiter return to the bar and whisper something to a small woman with a severe strawberry blonde bob who is polishing wine glasses. The woman nods and laughs dismissively as she holds a glass up to the light for inspection. The truth would give both of you something really juicy to gossip about she thinks as she swallows more champagne.

She looks through the window and meets her gaze in a thick blackness punctuated by city lights. The image is distorted by ribbons of rain unravelling down the glass. But she recognises herself. Recognises that there is neither distortion nor doubt within her now. The restaurant door opens and street noises tumble across the threshold. She continues to silently converse with her reflection, not turning to see who has entered as she's certain it isn't him. He won't make the effort to try to reach her sooner because she knows exactly why he's late. She has always chosen never to confront him with the truth. Why should she be the one to unlock his Pandora's Box of excuses, falsehoods, shams and deceits? The illicit treasure of lies that hide within are his to surrender.

The deception took hold about a year ago at the kind of social event that frequents their international working lives. Hectic schedules meant they had travelled separately, she arriving early as the evening was being hosted by her firm. Recent professional commitments had taken her away from home for longer periods than usual so she wanted to look particularly captivating for her husband that night.

Appearance has always been something of tremendous pride and importance to her. She wore a beautiful new three-quarter length Ceylon sapphire-blue dress with matching shoes. It had looked so splendid, so full of expectation as it hung in her bedroom that afternoon. Waves of soft, cool, silk poured over her skin when she put on the dress. She admired her finished work in the mirror. A worthwhile investment, she thought. The alabaster complexion of her youth may have departed but what replaced it was still, she thought, very desirable.

He always knew how to make an entrance and when he walked into the champagne reception he'd looked as handsome as always in dinner suit and black tie. She'd had a few seconds to watch the tall, distinguished figure of her husband as he accepted a drink from a waiter before scanning the room in search of her. He would pause, like a highly-acclaimed actor waiting for his audience to applaud his performance. She used to love watching people cease from talking and drinking to admire him as he moved among them; felt a powerful thrill, knowing that she was the magnet drawing his attention away from everyone else and towards her.

The early years, as they discovered each other and as their careers flourished, were exciting. At the most inappropriate time, usually during a long, dull speech, he would place his hand in the small of her back and whisper into her ear how gorgeous she looked, how he couldn't wait to take her home. Then there were the expensive holidays, cars and restaurants, skiing trips, the villa in Provence and the appropriate and well-connected friends. And with such a busy and demanding lifestyle, there was never talk of having children. But the wealth of rewards and the trinkets of professional success gradually lost their sheen as the years blindly accelerated towards an inevitable landscape of complacency.

A double decker bus stops in a queue of traffic outside the restaurant. Two young girls wave and blow kisses at her while their mother looks at her phone. She, however, doesn't notice the performance; doesn't see the bus edge forward beyond the window frame boundary of her vision. It is another scene that plays out in front of her.

Would the current circumstances be different if she had not left him chatting with guests that evening while she crossed the room to speak to a new client? It was a short journey, a brief period of separation, but enough for someone else to fill the space at his side. *If only he'd come with me* - a useless thought that had often visited her before departing to torture another restless, searching conscience elsewhere. Perhaps she could have prevented the momentary seismic shift that realigned their worlds. But such retrospection offered her a shatterproof window through which she viewed a life that could have been.

You'll be astonished that I know, she thinks, as she adjusts the polished silver dinner knife lying on the white linen tablecloth. *But I'm trained to notice everything. I know you better than you can ever imagine. Your behaviours, attitudes, habits, moods, preferences, dislikes. The slightest change and I sense it immediately. The way you looked at her as you used to look at me. The way you laughed and talked with her as we used to laugh and talk. You even danced, and with an energy I've not witnessed for a long time, if ever. Did she remind you of my younger self? Of the years before life started to dismantle me?*

So many faceless people and forgotten conversations swam around me as I observed you over shoulders or across the dining table. And I watched, helpless, as you began to slip away from me, while I laughed too enthusiastically with colleagues, drank too much red wine.

A waiter walks past her carrying two plates but their warm aromas do nothing to arouse her hunger. It is altogether a different appetite that drives her towards repletion. She watches the orange light of a taxi switch off as a man gets into the vehicle and is driven somewhere beyond the heart of the city.

They'd taken a taxi home from the reception that night. It was only a short journey to their house but the distance between them grew to be immense. Two minds wrestling with separate thoughts of a husband drifting away and a potential lover racing nearer. Two hearts whose emotions crashed around in the silent vacuum of the black cab that drove them towards a junction where futures would splinter and crack.

As she finishes her champagne, she recalls him offering her a drink when they'd arrived home. Her head had felt as though it was being squeezed in a vice. She'd declined on the grounds of a long and exhausting day and instead made herself some camomile tea. He poured a large glass of whiskey for himself while she looked through the mail. She examined his reflection in the glass patio doors as she pretended to read a letter.

There was a new nervousness about him as he refilled the tumbler, glanced at his watch and smoothed back his silvering hair. The holiday in Jamaica that she'd booked earlier that day now seemed so inappropriate. She'd intended to surprise him when they reached home but the words clung to the inside her throat.

Neither of them could find anything else to say. Both of them wanted to be elsewhere. Suddenly he remembered he needed to make an important business call to New York. She caught a few words about not waiting up and time differences as he disappeared into his study and shut the door.

Later, while she lay in bed, staring into the isolating blackness, a finger of moonlight slipped through the shutters and stroked the blue dress that had been discarded in the corner of the bedroom. The shoes lay in separate places of exile, lost somewhere among the shadows on the cream wool carpet.

She'd listened to the hushed voice downstairs as the deception started to bury its roots deep within his heart. Tears gathered on her pillow, tiny pools of anguish in which her marriage slowly started to sink. When he eventually joined her in their bed, neither word nor touch was offered as he turned away from her. They lay awake, two hearts desperately beating out the contrasting rhythms of grief and excitement against their ribs. Back-to-back, only she felt the pressure of the widening chasm that would force them asunder.

The restaurant door opens. This time she senses it is him. The force of the door being shut, a cough, the pace of footsteps – all these are referenced deep within her. She hears the polite conversation between him and the head waiter – a few words of apology, some laughter, the exchanges of men who understand each other. She waits for him to join her.

For months she has been watching and waiting; erecting and tearing down her obstacles of denial; fighting both the anger that would erupt without warning, and the ensuing depression that tried to bury her. Trying to manage her emotions was like spinning plates. She couldn't let one slip otherwise they'd all come crashing down, along with her career and her self-respect. There were so many times when she wanted to scream at him, confront him, hurt him.

Perhaps she should have played his game and looked elsewhere. Men still made it very clear that they found her attractive. But she hadn't wanted to increase the risk of losing him to someone else. Her sharp-bladed ruthlessness, cultivated throughout years of fighting for professional recognition, couldn't administer to her terrifying fear of betrayal and loneliness.

Then, last New Year, as time journeyed towards a new decade, it delivered an alternative perspective to her as it wandered through the night. An unfamiliar voice slipped into her subconscious and repeatedly asked the question, 'Is this helping you or is this harming you?' She woke early with the understanding that the man lying next to her was not essential to her existence; that she was not prepared to make compromises that permitted his infidelity. Her loss would be more than balanced by rediscovering a life free from the despair she had tried and failed to suppress.

Now he is beside her at the table. He bends down to kiss her forehead and repeats his well- rehearsed excuses and apologies as he sits down and unfolds his napkin. More words are spoken at her and more champagne arrives along with the menus. His words pass through her as she reaches down to touch the soft leather briefcase containing the photographs and report from a private investigator.

Reassured and smiling, she sips her champagne while the fingers of her right hand spread across her lap and the cool silk folds of her blue dress. The waiting is nearly over and she is ready to force his secret out into the open, to hear the confession that will expose him. Opportunity is the companion she now desires.

No winter lasts forever

He stands beside the teacher's desk and watches the eyes of the children staring at him. They sit in groups around shiny-topped tables. In his old school, he and his friends sat in rows that were divided by a central aisle. At the start of the school day, they would laugh and chat in the classroom, with someone positioned at the door as a lookout for the teacher. They would be in trouble if they did not stand up for him as soon as he entered the room.

No one had stood up today and the teacher had to tell the children to be quiet. While she takes the register, he tries and fails to read the expression on the pale moon faces in front of him. They all look the same. It is only the different hair lengths and colours that define them as individuals. Behind them, the walls are covered in brightly coloured pictures and symbols he doesn't recognise.

The teacher is speaking but he cannot understand what she is saying except when he hears his name. His heart beat sprints beneath an itchy, unfamiliar vest and he resists wiping his sweaty palms against his grey polyester trousers. Next to him is a strange-looking plant in a small tin bucket. Its green leaves have burst out of a ball that has broken through the surface of the soil. A sturdy stem shoots upwards, supporting a large towering flower displaying a multitude of petals in star formations.

Their intense blueness reminds him of a head covering his mother used to wear when family and friends came to dinner. He can taste the plant's powerful scent and now a hint of nausea pokes at the fear and anxiety that have been jostling for attention in his stomach since the early morning. He hopes he won't be standing here for much longer.

45

The teacher stops speaking and the children slowly say something together then clap their hands. He wonders if he should also clap his hands but he is too nervous to do anything. He'd really like to scratch the back of his neck where his shirt collar is rubbing against his skin. The long piece of cloth that was knotted beneath the collar that morning by the lady he is staying with feels like a lump pressing against his throat. But not as big as the lump that has lodged inside his throat, and tried to choke him for months. His black jumper matches those worn by the boys and girls in the class but it smells of someone else. Before he came here, his mother used to wash and starch his uniform every evening, ready for the next day. He would get up with the sun and walk to school with his friends in a cloud of perfumed cleanliness.

He feels the teacher's gentle hand against his back as she guides him between the tables. He looks down at the patterned wooden floor, listening to his black shoes squeaking against its surface. He has known so many different floors: the smooth tiles of his grandmother's house, the cold rubber dampness of the tiny boat in which everyone had been sick, the hard lorry floor he had slept on. As the vehicle tossed and bumped him towards his fate, tears of fear and loneliness stopped only when hunger forced him into unconsciousness. The filth in his corner of the lorry and the stench of diesel fumes clung to his nostrils for weeks after his journey had ended.

The empty plastic chair that awaits him is bright orange with a texture similar to the fruit's skin. He loves oranges. He used to go to the market with his mother to buy them. She would fill her string bags with fruit, vegetables, herbs and spices, while the rich aromas from the food stalls - freshly-made flatbreads ready for dipping in muhammara sauce, juicy chicken shawarmas, sweet pastries filled with sugar syrup and roasted pistachios - would tempt them as they passed through the narrow alleyways.

He struggles to eat the food in his new home. Breakfast comes out of a cardboard box with milk from another box poured over it. Dinner is often scraped out of a metal carton and heated up in a microwave. Neither the smell nor the taste of anything he eats conveys what it is. He hopes the food will be better in this school. He is always very hungry.

He sits down in front of a large piece of white paper. Two plastic boxes of jewel-coloured crayons are in the middle of the table.

The teacher sits next to him. *She is too big for this chair*, he thinks, as he stares at her enormous knees protruding from the hem of her dress. She points a finger at her chest and says something. He watches her lips, hears her voice. Then she points at him and says his name. She keeps repeating these movements and sounds until eventually he understands that she is saying her name. He holds it in his memory, ready for the time when he is able to speak to the world again. She smells soft and fresh, not like the intoxicating plant that stands to attention on her desk. She touches the paper and points at the box of crayons then moves on to another table.

There are four other boys and one girl at his table. The girl is sitting next to him and as he bends over the sheet of paper his eyes slide sideways. He has never seen hair like hers and it reminds him of the mounds of curly burnt sugar strands with which his mother would decorate some of her homemade sweets. The skin beneath the tiny orange dots scattered across the girl's nose and cheeks is milk-white.

The boys glance across at him then share whispers and giggles with each other when they think the teacher isn't looking. He can't understand them, even though his hearing has recovered from the deafening destruction of endless bombing. He knows they are talking about him and nascent tears sting his eyes while a hot despair sweeps across his face.

He looks to his right where a window frames the scrubbed-grey sky and the silhouette of an early-budding tree. Rain hits the glass as though desperate to enter the warmth and shelter of the classroom. The horrid, angry, inhospitable weather has shadowed him everywhere in this new country. He wants to go home, to his real home with his parents, sister, grandparents, the lazy cat on the roof, the lizard that snoozes beneath the giant pot that sits outside the washhouse and overflows with his mother's herbs. But the house was destroyed and his family and pets were killed. They exist only as memories of a past to which there is no return. Occasionally they appear to him in a dream, a brief respite from his recurrent nightmares and the smell of death that lingers until the early morning.

Something touches him. He turns to see the girl's small fingers resting on his forearm. In her other hand she offers him a fistful of crayons. He looks into her sea-green eyes that are fixed upon him. She smiles and her freckles perform a little dance. He takes the crayons and she shifts around in her seat to return to the picture she is drawing. It is a house with a tall chimney, big windows and a wide-open door. A bright orange sun with red and yellow rays rises into a cloudless sky beneath her swirling crayons. His old house is a pile of rubble and he can't remember what his new one looks like.

The other boys are drawing rockets, cars, guns and monsters in dark colours and big gestures. He looks at his gift of crayons lying like a broken rainbow next to the paper. As he searches his memory for a suitable image, he rubs his nose and notices that his fingers smell of the candles his grandmother used to burn after sunset. Their intoxicating aromas would drift through the house long after they had been extinguished, the strongest ones still discernible when the old cockerel announced daybreak.

He picks up a black crayon, holds it over the paper for a few seconds then puts it back on the table. Another heavy shower of rain splatters across the window and he looks up to see skeletal branches being tortured by an invisible force. His index finger wanders between the crayons until he picks up a green one and starts to draw. Other colours gradually spread across the page as he loses himself in the process of his creativity.

The little girl leans across to look at what he is doing and she puts two thumbs up at him. He smiles as she gives him her bright blue crayon, and he knows that it will be the perfect colour for the plant's galaxy of star-shaped petals.

Cleaning in progress

If God existed, he'd invite me to sit beside his beautiful, almighty right hand. *Come closer, Chrissie*, he'd say. I'd be so close to his godliness's throne. So close that I could whisper in his ear. We'd exchange opinions on cleanliness; it's an important subject for him – I learned that at Sunday School. He surely would praise my expertise. But God is a myth. Such a shame as I'd love to show him my studio.

In here, everything has its place. And today, like every other day, each pristine item is in its pristine place. Just how I like it. Exactly as I arranged it last night before I closed. Everything is sterilized. It's all been through the sterilizer, the autoclave. And I always sterilize the autoclave.

Now for my morning checks. Go through it all again before I open. Biohazard containers ready to receive anything that encounters blood and bodily fluids. Sharps containers for old needles. Loads of those. Don't want those getting lost. Sink scrubbed, taps polished, nothing lingering in the plughole. I'll just wash my hands again. Apply a generous squirt of approved antibacterial handwash. Always wipe down the bottle after use. And there's another worry. How to sterilize the approved antibacterial handwash. There are no guidelines. An approved antibacterial hand wipe is my current strategy.

The disposable gloves are essential. Cross contamination - it's a nightmare. But I must keep on top of things, keep it all clean, clean, clean. Single use disposable gloves. The signs are everywhere: HAVE YOU REMEMBERED YOUR GLOVES? Upper case, Arial Black – the font was a difficult decision – the question screams at me from behind the easy-to-wipe laminate. So many pairs for each client. Gloves on, off, on, off. Hundreds of daily percussive snap-twangs smacking the air. New gloves, clean the equipment, new gloves, touch the skin, new gloves, position the stencil, new gloves, touch the machine, new gloves, tattoo the skin, new gloves, clean the wound. And then the special clear plastic for skin areas not being tattooed but which I might touch with my disposable gloves. Which I must dispose of. In the sterilized disposable glove container. Which has been in the autoclave.

I wanted to be a great artist. I couldn't believe it when I won a scholarship to the best art college in London. I celebrated with my parents in the Italian restaurant on the High Street. Dad and the owner were Freemasons, so we always went to Luciano's on family occasions. Dad almost managed to hide his disappointment during dinner. But as we waited for the bill, he gave me the look. The one I'd seen repeatedly demolish my mother for years.

There was always a shard of hatred in the look. A brief glint and then it was thrust in, hard and sharp. A lightning flash before the destructive storm. He'd expected me, his only child, to go to university, pursue a professional career. Art student wasn't suitable for upholding his Masonic lodge aura of respectability. But I had defied him and there was nothing he could do about it. Nothing, at least, that he could do to me.

I rode the path of defiance all the way to art school and found Jackson at the end of it. Jackson had spent several years travelling and working in south-east Asia, Australia and New Zealand. The other guys on the course were fresh from the classroom: a collection of gangly, uncommunicative, schoolboys, all dressed in the dark uniform that screamed anti-establishment cool art student. Jackson's thick, black ponytail, and his strong, tanned body beneath faded jeans, T-shirts and a biker's leather jacket were matched by his confidence. I wasn't the only one who noticed him. But when he showed an enthusiastic interest in me and my art, I didn't think life could get any better.

Buried deep into each other and into our work, he introduced me to body modification. Tattoos. Everyone's got them now but back then they were still that rare symbol of rebellion. Jackson had a beautiful blue dolphin, about six inches long, tattooed on his upper left arm, the arm he always put around me. The dolphin swam when Jackson flexed his muscles.

'Did you know that all tattoos have hidden meanings, Chrissie?'

'And the dolphin?'

'Living in two worlds at once, a creature of water, a breather of air.'

I only needed one world inhabited by the two of us.

My first tattoo was a spider's web. I feared how painful it might be as I presented my arm. I couldn't watch Jackson working at the lacy black image on my right wrist. Just beneath it, my pulse panicked, thumping the table as though trapped within the delicate inky strands. I listened to the hum of the tattoo pen and tried not to resist the unfamiliar sensations of pricking and numbness. This was interrupted by Jackson dabbing the tiny blood bubbles like little ruby stones. Then I dared myself to witness my skin's transformation and for the first time in my life, I came alive. I woke up. This was where I wanted to be. This was art.

'Captured in my web forever,' he whispered as he kissed my hot cheek.

Dad called me a slut when he saw what I had done. Tattoos were for deviants, prisoners, bikers, thugs, prostitutes. Nothing wrong with my family, though. Respectable, middle-class, car cleaned every Sunday, house and garden presented to showroom standard, life memberships at the Conservative bowling club and the golf club. Nothing wrong with my Dad talking to his best mate at the bottom of a whisky tumbler then using my Mum to purge his self-loathing. Slapping, punching, kicking.

By the time I left home I knew his entire repertoire. Learned it by heart as it filtered through my bedroom wall. Then there was the occasional cigarette burn on Mum's arm when Dad perhaps didn't like the dinner she'd prepared, or she'd dared to offer an opinion. His creativity flourished throughout their marriage. Perhaps that's where I got it from. Now that would really have pissed him off. Yes, Mum knew all about body modification. She carried the marks of status and rank, her very own decorations for bravery, her rewards for devotion.

We only spoke about it once. I was home for a few days at the end of my first year in college. Mum didn't usually wear much make up but I could just distinguish the marbling beneath the thick layer of foundation, blusher and powder.

'You shouldn't have to put up with him anymore, Mum.'

She turned away from me and scrubbed the immaculate kitchen sink. A bracelet of swirling purple bruises danced around her wrist. 'You don't understand, Chrissie.'

I reached out and touched her shoulder, my spider's web emerging from beneath my shirt sleeve. 'Why don't you come away with me?'

She pulled back. 'Just leave it, OK?'

I left it and I left her with that merciless monster. My discovery of body art awoke me to a kaleidoscope of choice. But what choice did she have? She didn't design the pattern of scars on her body, didn't choose the permanent imprints on her skin, nor the carvings on her soul. Bruises of imprisonment, cigarette burns of emptiness; the long thin knife cut above her left eye, the blade of hatred twisting in her heart. I read somewhere that the Romans used to tattoo, "Stop me, I'm a runaway," on their slaves' foreheads. My Dad should have had, "Stop me, I'm a wife-beater," chiselled into his.

My life with Jackson was unimaginably exciting. Together we unlocked one another's unlimited creativity, complemented one another, produced fantastic art. Our tutors loved it, encouraged it. Our fellow students hated it, resented it. But we didn't care.

Making great art led to great to sex which inspired even greater art. Sex with Jackson was something else to get excited about. None of the embarrassing cheap alcohol-fuelled fumblings reminiscent of Freshers' Week. Oh no. Jackson was relaxed and attentive, carefully exploring my body, stroking my skin. Every tiny molecule was ignited by his touch. Messages fired like bullets to the core of my desire. I think he was mapping me, locating and recording every area that responded to him. By the time he fucked me I was lost, my mind disconnected from my body, my subconscious rising to the bait of visceral instinct.

I didn't need any other friends and definitely not my parents. Scratched everyone out of my life. Jackson was all I craved. He was skilled in keeping my dosage levels topped up. Unveiled so many artistic possibilities by tapping into my subconscious with mind-altering drink and drugs.

We dropped out of art college. Jackson said we didn't need it. Our body art designs were brilliant and were gaining recognition. Highly acclaimed for their originality. None of the hearts and angels and butterflies sentimentality. I can always recognize the women who want these before they've shut my studio door. Something to complement the radical fortieth birthday belly button piercing.

The affirmation tattoo is very popular at the moment. Vacuous words providing the answers to middle-aged malaise. *"The best of us can find happiness in misery."* Why? *"That which does not kill me makes me stronger."* Mum disproved that theory. I had a beauty last year. *"NIGEL – here is the root of the root and the bud of the bud and the sky of the sky of a tree called life which grows higher than the soul can hope or the mind can hide and this is the wonder that's keeping the stars apart. I carry your heart, I carry it in my heart."* Her first tattoo. All over her left arm. She threw the cheating bastard out last month.

No. Our work was much better than the rubbish I reproduce. The back was our favoured canvas as we specialized in large, 3D images. Mythical creatures that clung to the neck and wrapped themselves around the waist. Fiery Chinese warriors and Japanese warlords. Religious perspectives - Christian, Pagan, Hindu, Islamic, Judaic. Ancient Polynesian tribal designs. Whole new blazing worlds of colour and pattern created in our heads and transcribed onto human flesh. Incredible. Our first studio was called 'Irezumi,' after the Japanese word for 'insertion of ink.' Tattooists and clients loved us. We had exhibitions. We were global.

We didn't have many tattoos on our bodies because we knew we'd want to remove them, change them. Like re-hanging pictures in a gallery. Far too painful. But Jackson liked experimenting with pens, pencils and paint. He'd sketch designs on me. It was a convenient and effective way of seeing how the ink pattern would appear on the skin. I found it quite relaxing and often erotic. I was his tattoo muse. His inspiration. I would lie for hours as he drew all over my body. I wasn't allowed to speak, to move, to barely breathe.

In the zone he was outstanding. When he slipped outside it, he was brutal. I felt the frustration of his slaps and punches where the pattern or pigment was all wrong. I became a piece of dehumanized artistic kit. Sometimes he would press the pen or pencil hard into my skin, piercing it, leaving traces of ink or graphite beneath the surface. When the pain was too much, my screams would rouse him from his creative reverie and he would hug me, sobbing and apologetic, tears stinging my wounds, the rainbow smudges collecting in the hollows of my collar bones.

I became Jackson's addiction. I nourished his genius. And I could reproduce his designs. His life would have disintegrated without me. But I was powerless; frightened of not being needed. Trapped in a world where love had been pushed into a deep, dark chasm by his psychotic desire for self-fulfilment, for an unachievable perfection. I was the lucky charm, the talisman, the essential travelling companion on this neurotic journey. I had purpose; I was needed. It's what we all want, isn't it?

He suggested a research trip to the Cook Islands. It was here, in the eighteenth century, that the Polynesians had introduced tattooing to maritime explorers. Jackson wanted us to work in this environment, take inspiration from it, allow its history to pierce and renew our art. My mind and body, being the deliverer and recipient respectively of creativity, were exhausted. I was desperate for anything that might offer a new direction in our lives.

I booked a small, isolated lodge on the island of Aitutaki. We hired a scooter at the airport and puttered away with our supplies in search of it. We arrived to find the key in the lock and a piece of paper announcing 'Welcome Chrissie,' pinned to the wooden door. That evening I walked barefoot on the soft white sand and listened to the ocean's songs. Holding Jackson's hand, I felt a reconnection with the only man I have ever loved.

At first, we slept a lot, waking to have slow, indulgent sex, take a gentle swim or a walk, to eat and drink. And we laughed. Repeatedly, for the first time in ages. Then Jackson started to read and sketch, becoming so distracted that he didn't notice my long absences on walks or scooter rides. But I didn't mind. The island revealed her beauty to me borne in her fragile coral reef, endless beaches and fertile vegetation. Aitutaki began to heal my surface wounds and cleanse my damaged spirit.

I returned early one evening to find Jackson drunk, his eyes flaming with determination. His sour breath stung my face as he slurred through terrifying descriptions of the primitive tattooing techniques previously used by the ancient tribes of this area. Cutting into the skin the symbols of fertility, the marks of protection; inserting amulets of spiritual devotion and then rubbing the wounds with ashes from a sacred bonfire.

'And I must experiment with the ritual of hand tapping ink under the skin through hollowed sticks or animal bones,' he said.

I couldn't find my voice. I drank several bottles of warm beer, listening to him describe how beautiful I'd look, how we must begin immediately.

'Let's wait until tomorrow,' I finally managed. 'I've found the perfect place.'

As I watched Jackson put away the weird selection of tattooing tools and materials he'd hidden in his rucksack, my cold skin shivered in the warm evening. Jackson slid into the uninterrupted sleep of the drunkard. I sat on the verandah and followed the black night's journey towards the pink glowing resolve of dawn that settled on my body.

That morning, I led him to the perfect place: an elevated area, long ago inhabited by natives. Jackson's wide smile told me he loved it.

'We can commune with the ancient spirits to enrich our creativity,' I said as I spread a blanket on the grass. Inquisitive breezes dashed in and out of the forest to tease the tiny hairs on my arms and neck. A thunderous waterfall drowned out the sound of blood screaming in my ears. Jackson stood at the ravine's edge and raised his arms as if waiting to catch the sun.

The swallow, a symbol of hope that I had tattooed on his shoulder, appeared to flap its wings over the shifting sinews and flesh. I watched my hand pick up one of Jackson's knives and stab the bird in the heart. Jackson tried to turn but my hand just kept stabbing at his beautiful body, the dark red blood flowing down the groove of his spine as he arched his back.

'Chrissie!'

The ticklish progress of an orange ladybird across my knuckles woke me. I had no idea how long it had been since the world had dissolved. When I opened my eyes the heat of the afternoon filled the space where Jackson had stood. I gazed into the argument of foaming white water in the gorge far below me. I breathed slowly, deeply.

When I came home, I sold our studio and our work. It was easy. Everything was in my name because I had always looked after our business, always been the organiser. Clients were sorry that we'd split up because of our artistic differences. I was sorry not to be able to tell them where he was. But that was so typical of Jackson.

There was much sympathy for my distress but also an understanding of Jackson's need to reinvent his creative self. It was so easy to add the artistry of deceit to my portfolio. So easy to wipe Jackson away.

My creativity is long dead. Reproducing someone else's work suits me now. I'm skilled, quick and efficient. Being in the zone helps me forget, stops my hands shaking, stops me craving a drink.

The move to this town is my sixth attempt at making a clean start. I just can't seem to settle. People always want to get to know you. Plenty of clients, each one departing with all manner of self-expression pulsating beneath the sterilized protective covering. My first one today is a dream-catcher. Beautiful rich colours. Nape of the neck. Obstructs evil while allowing goodness to enter.

I could have discussed this principle with God. Offered him his tattoo of choice.

Concentrate, Chrissie. Check the inks are strong enough.
Tattoos can fade with age. They sink deeper into the skin's dermis. Where my life must have gone. My tattered soul trapped within layers of damaged tissue. Some wounds never heal. Gloves on. Wipe the surfaces one more time. Wipe it all away.

Something old, something new

She fills his glass. He raises it.

'Congratulations, Debs. Thirty years, who'd believe it, eh? Not such a life sentence after all.'

Debs smiles and then drains her glass before pouring herself some more champagne. She takes a sip, enjoying the bubbly fireworks on her tongue. Harry is still speaking but his words are lost in the din of city bosses kicking off the weekend party. Her husband's fat lips open and close before her like an overfed goldfish and she offers the occasional nod of disinterested recognition.

Debs is comfortable in these surroundings. She knows that Harry would rather be in The Lazy Frog with his real ales and his quiz or darts teams, or in the Supporters' Lounge with his mates after the football. She's always encouraged him in his interests, especially when a tournament or an away match has taken him further afield and has offered her the promise of a few nights in her own company.

Harry Patterson. Has she really lived with this man for thirty years? *I've actually known him for thirty-three*, she thinks as she delicately skewers another pitted black olive with a cocktail stick. As she places the olive in her mouth, she admires her professionally buffed and finished fingernails. Too Hot To Handle. Her manicurist had told her it was simply the perfect colour for a special occasion like this one.

Harry thought she was hot when he first met her. It all began with a few words exchanged during the evening tea breaks at the polytechnic. He was a trainee plumber and she was grappling with book- keeping. Harry consumed a lot of weak tea and bourbon biscuits before finally asking her out. Now, sitting in this central London bar, Debs tries to recall some fragment of that first date.

There was definitely a meal in an Italian restaurant with red checked table cloths and lights on big black curly wires that could be adjusted above the heads of couples to create a more, or perhaps less, romantic atmosphere. She laughed too much when Harry banged his head on the glass lampshade as he stood up to leave.

They may have seen a film after that, possibly The Long Good Friday. Or perhaps that was with Paul or Andrew or that teacher who admired her neat cash flow columns and her long legs.

The pink leather case containing her iPhone shudders across the wooden table in the direction of a row of tea lights sparkling in little glass jars. She grabs the device, delighted to see her daughter's name light up.

'Hang on a mo, Harry. It's a text from Karen.'

Holding the phone almost at arm's length, she can just make out her daughter's message. *God, the light's bad in here*, she thinks.

'Everything alright, Debs?'

Ignoring her husband's question, Debs' eyes skitter across the text like skimming-stones bouncing over water. As she finishes reading, the breath gripped high in her chest escapes from her flared nostrils in a triumphant sigh. Debs enjoys the few seconds of sole ownership before sharing the news in an uncontrollable crescendo of excitement.

'She's done it. She's beaten those bloody chauvinists and got herself the top job in Dubai! I bet they can't believe it. She leaves next week. I knew it, I just knew she'd do it!'

Harry opens his mouth to speak but Debs isn't interested. She raises her arm and a jangle of gold bracelets summons a whey-faced, spiky-haired youth to the table. He leans in as Debs whispers a few brief words into his ear while gently squeezing his hand. She can sense the heat of his embarrassment on her face. Smiling, she watches the student, who is uncomfortably occupying the outfit of a larger waiter, as he slopes away with her champagne order.

Her gaze drifts from following his slim hips to surveying the sea of bespoke, pin-striped suits that fill the expensively converted bank. She resists the urge to leap onto her chair and scream the news of her achievement at them. To proudly declare that Karen

Patterson will lead the life she deserves. A very different life from the one that Deborah Patterson chose.

Harry had affectionately called her Debs from the very beginning. At first, she liked the idea of being married to the strong, quiet plumber. He was her ticket to a secure and comfortable life, a fortuitous escape from the tiny terraced house she shared with her parents and two brothers. Harry worked hard to build a company with a strong reputation and a wealthy client list. Initially, Debs looked after the business accounts and they were richly rewarded with all the trappings of success that she had desired.

When Karen was born, Debs passed her work onto a firm of accountants recommended by a personal financial advisor. She didn't think life could get any better. And in a way, she was right. The new family had it all and it was living the dream: the detached house with all the latest fittings, wardrobes full of designer clothes, private gym membership, expensive holidays, two cars, swimming pool, even pedigree cats.

Something else happened when Karen was born, an occurrence so small that it passed unnoticed at first. A tiny seed was sown that grew, very, very slowly, into a large, empty void. It seemed to push Harry and Debs further and further apart. Harry loved his family and immersed himself in his flourishing business in order to maintain a comfortable lifestyle. Debs also loved her family and the riches her husband could provide.

But money couldn't buy the passion, couldn't build the emotional bridge that was missing between husband and wife and which Debs so desperately needed. Motherhood offered her the opportunity to invest her love, ambition and energy in a project that would help her forget, or at least manage to live with, her own shortcomings. Debs stopped searching for the parts of her she had mislaid long ago, just like the absent letters in her name.

Someone seems to have turned the Muzak up and the lights down. Friday evening is officially up and running. Debs is loving every moment of it. Even Harry looks better in this light and at least she doesn't have to listen to what he's saying. She blames the champagne for his uncharacteristic chattiness. When Harry finally stops talking, Debs watches her husband clumsily texting with his thick fingers which are almost too large to press the keys individually. He hits the send button and offers his wife a massive grin. Debs forces a smile and twists around on her chair wondering why the waiter is taking so long.

As she does so, a tall, elegant woman in a long, tailored cashmere coat enters the bar. Debs admires her sophisticated silver sweep of expensively cut hair and the discreet glint of diamond earrings. *That will be me in ten years' time*, she muses. As she watches the woman confidently scanning the room, a sudden flush spreads across Debs' face and neck like a reckless red ink stain. The effects of excessive alcohol are all too common for Debs these days. Closing her eyes, she bows her forehead to meet the soothing coolness of her empty glass. The spinning top inside her skull clatters to a standstill and after a few minutes the heat subsides. By the time she recovers, someone has thankfully had the sense to change the Muzak to something a little more subdued.

'Are you alright, Debs?'

Debs looks up, pushing some damp strands of hair across her sweaty forehead. She stares expressionless at Harry's large face. He's now standing in front of her, hopefully about to leave her to enjoy the rest of her evening. He seems taller than usual and for the first time that day, she notices his unfamiliar Italian suit. She frowns, ignoring the first traces of a migraine and tries to comprehend the scene before her. Harry is holding the cashmere woman's hand and in return she bestows her perfect lipstick smile upon him.

Debs blinks once, twice but the image will not disappear. Harry's lips are still shaping sentences and now they begin to reach her ears as though someone is holding down the volume button on the television remote control. She stares back, her heart racing to its highest gear, her body rigid beneath her silk jacket. This is not how things are supposed to be.

'Sorry, Debs, but Patricia and I will have to rush. We don't want to be late for dinner and the show.'

She has no idea what he's talking about. In thirty-three years, Debs and Harry never went to the theatre.

'But a great idea of yours to celebrate the divorce today. You'll be so much happier with the house and everything.'

Debs opens her mouth but is incapable of uttering the words in her head.

'Talking this afternoon was such a relief. It didn't feel right telling you about Patricia until today. Tell Karen I'll be in touch, OK?'

Debs shakes the small right hand that is offered in front of her. The quality of the soft leather glove is unmistakable.

'So lovely to meet you, Deborah.'

Patricia's exquisitely carved syllables echo in Debs' head as her eyes track the two figures making their way through the crowd. Daylight tries and fails to sidle into the bar when the door opens onto the street. Then, in that moment, they are gone and she is left sitting alone in the dim shadows. Her incredulity is interrupted by a pale, nail-bitten hand placing a napkin and a single champagne flute before her.

'Would you like me to pour now, madam?'

Moira Harris

No fear, no surprise

Several hours ago, the longest day of the year rose from its brief slumber and rolled out a clean, blank canvas across the northern hemisphere. The awakening sun stretched and yawned, distilling its myriad palette of pink, red, orange and yellow pastels throughout the landscape. Flowers kissed by the nascent light unfurled themselves and stretched upwards in gratitude while birds performed well-rehearsed melodies to welcome the day. All life, both within and upon the earth, rock, and water of the majestic mountains, was charged with energy and expectancy.

Now, the approaching sound of a car engine interrupts the summer solitude. The sun observes the vehicle advancing along single-track road as it draws itself up into a bright golden sphere of warmth to embark upon its own journey across the unblemished azure sky. The stage is lit, the backdrop prepared, and the curtain rises on a black Audi estate car driving into the empty car park. The vehicle stops in a space beneath a large, ancient oak tree. The engine is turned off and silence is restored to the fresh, new summer air. The car sits like an unfamiliar guest among the gathering of trees and bushes that surrounds the car park.

The branches of the oak tree open wide like expanding lungs to inhale the morning breeze as it sways down the glen. Two crows crouched on opposite gate posts watch the tall, fair-haired man get out of the car and walk around to the back to open the boot. He removes a pair of sturdy, well-worn walking shoes and a pair of thick, bundled-up socks. An old green rucksack, carefully packed last night, leans against the first aid box. Being the practical type, he's always had one in the car, along with a tool kit, shovel, de-icer and emergency triangle. Essential when one lives in a rural

63

area, especially with difficult winter driving conditions. And not forgetting all the other possibilities one needs to be prepared for: breakdowns, accidents, illness. They can strike at any time.

Max changes his shoes and socks then grabs the rucksack. He hasn't been walking in the hills for a while and the rucksack feels heavy and unfamiliar as he lets it drop onto the gravel. The dark cavern of the empty boot stares back at him. Snapshots of what it used to contain on days like this leap out and hover in the air: more boots of different sizes, walking poles, a picnic basket, rainbow-coloured clothes, toys, a pushchair, some nappies.

He slams the car boot shut and the memories fly up and away into the sky along with the two startled crows. Max presses both his palms, slim fingers spread wide, against the car's dusty bodywork and shakes his head between his outstretched arms. He takes a few deep breaths before standing upright to check his mobile phone. Eager eyes scan the screen for text messages or missed calls. The faint signal dies but there's nothing there for him.

Max looks at the ground, kicking the gravel so hard that some of the loose chippings ricochet off the oak's broad trunk. Several branches seem to wave their leafy fists in protest. He shoves the phone back into his trouser pocket and raises his eyes to consider the task before him. Two shimmering reflections of the mountain settle upon the mirrored lenses of his sunglasses. Max surveys the familiar panorama but today it seems somehow different. He feels like a lost child being taken back to his home. The bleep of his digital watch interrupts these thoughts and reminds him why he's here. Max locks the car, drags the rucksack onto his back and sets off.

The empty car park suggests to Max that he is first on the mountain path. This is exactly what he wants. It's early enough for surprised walkers to see him striding down from the ridge later on while they are still on their way up. Or perhaps Max won't meet anyone else as he's planned a new route off the mountain today. His boots crunch along the path he has trodden many times. The first section is well maintained and wide enough for two people to walk comfortably side by side.

He used to think that this lulled walkers into a false sense of security; that the ascent would be gradual and easy under foot all the way to the top. But he knows that about a third of the way up, the thin scattering of birch and pine vanishes and the wide gravel path narrows to one that is steep and rocky. It's the point at which local dog walkers turn around. Max hasn't reached that point yet but he is already breathing hard.

Sweat stings his half-closed eyes as he propels his leaden limbs up the still gentle slope. The rucksack bites into his shoulders like a wild animal trying to drag him back to the car and Max accepts his fitness is not as good at it used to be. But there is a steeliness in his solitary figure on the mountain today; a determination that drives him forward without question or hesitation.

Mindful of his discomfort, Max shifts his focus from himself to the enveloping landscape. *You can only live in the moment*, whispers a voice inside his head. And as he steps from one moment to the next, his inquisitive senses rush from his body like excited children and return with precious treasures: jewels of shimmering quartzite embedded in the rock, a lyrical skylark serenading its mate without pausing for breath, a warm air that plays in his hair and prickles his skin, caresses his lips. The air delivers the summer perfumes of intoxicating yellow gorse flowers, warm pine, even a hint of gin from the juniper scrub.

Max stops to pick a handful of bilberries then continues onwards. The intense sharpness of the fruit stings his mouth just as it had done when he was a boy. As a young man, he had brought some of his girlfriends up here to pick the tiny berries. Sometimes, purple-stained lips and fingers had exchanged kisses, explored bodies. The route became a kind of initiation test. Being someone inclined to plan ahead, it was no surprise that Max compiled a secret list of attributes for his future wife. Top of this list was a love of the outdoors and walking in hills and mountains. Many tried and failed while others refused.

But then she appeared. On their first walk she almost sprinted to the trig point, then asked which was the next summit they were to head for. They'd spent ten hours in the mountains that day. Later on, in the pub, she'd ticked another box with her impressive knowledge and consumption of malt whiskies. Finally, in bed that night, she'd shared her philosophy of life with Max: no fear, no surprise, no hesitation, no doubt. It was the basis of her work as a professional life coach. How could he resist this woman who was qualified to encourage people to embrace life? He loved the philosophy as much as he loved her and it became the belief system that guided them almost to the end.

The crunch of gravel disappears from beneath Max's feet as the gently traversing path narrows and starts to climb up a rocky ravine. Now he must concentrate on foot placement to maintain his balance and avoid tripping over. He's always loved walking, finding and adjusting his rhythm to suit the pace that the terrain demands; getting beyond the initial twenty-minute battle with leg muscles warming up, lungs burning, heart raging to circulate blood and oxygen. The reward, a strong dose of endorphins to enhance the magnificence of a landscape bursting with possibility. On a clear, summer's day like today, there's nothing to match it.

How marvellous it would be, he used to think, to be able to prescribe the outdoor experience as a course of treatment for his patients. Over the years, Max has listened to many stories of unhappiness, unfulfillment, tragedy, misery, depression and anxiety. One by one, people sitting opposite him, ignorant of what they need yet desperate to find answers or at least a clue to help them avoid the dead ends in the black mazes that imprison them.

These people aren't identified by clothing, language, accent, behaviour, weight, choice of newspaper or TV programme. Their illness is a skilled and cunning master of disguise. No, the lowest common denominator is often a translucent white pallor, hands and faces like mottled pastry.

Max is quick to recognise troubled souls who dwell in bleak inner spaces and have not sought the healing distraction of simple fresh air for a long time, if at all. He's good at his job. He knows that the mind, like the body, needs care and nourishment. Its health and well-being are fundamental to an individual's quality of life, to that person's very existence. But an illness that hides in the shadows of people's hearts is challenging to diagnose, to acquire funding for research and treatment, to convince society of the extent of its existence and consequences.

Max, therefore, doesn't always like discussing his work. He's learned to read people and has a good sense of how they will react before they've finished asking the question. A therapist? Really? How interesting. If Max manages to produce the three words, Cognitive Behavioural Therapy, before reference is made to people being too soft these days or the unhealthy influence of America on our society, it's a small victory.

Although hot and thirsty, Max pushes on, afraid of what he might think or do if he stops. The stream hurtles downhill beside him, white foam falling over itself in a race to arrive at the bottom. Smooth, rounded boulders anchored in the middle of the current offer no obstacles to the ice-cold torrent. His heart beat, buried beneath too many layers of technical clothing, thumps harder and faster. Little bubbles of sweat edge down his temples while others burst and descend his spine in moist threads to collect in the small of his back.

As he continues his upward battle, Max concentrates on keeping his shoulders back and chest open. His heavy breathing wheezes like the air in a pair of bellows as it is sucked deep to nudge at his abdomen then thrown back out into the world. He's mesmerised by the cyclic nature of this rhythmic life-force switching between his internal and external self, between darkness and light. But Max is focused, looking for a particular place, not stopping until he finds it. His eyes search ahead for a sharp left-hand bend in the path and then a dip where shelter can be sought on cold and windswept days.

He reaches the bend and stops when he sees the sculpted grey rock below him. The large lump of granite, weathered and eroded for many years, was toppled from its high home on the mountain and came to rest down there many years before. Two shallow indentations comfortably accommodate two people, side by side, either seated or lying down. Folklore tells of the Fairy Throne - a double love-throne for the king and queen of the mountain fairies. For mortals, however, it is the ideal place to share refreshments, secrets, kisses, desires, dreams. His dry lips form a crescent smile as memories of different times crowd into his racing mind.

Stepping down from the path, Max shrugs the rucksack off his aching shoulders and places it on the left-hand seat of the love-throne. He rolls the tension out of his shoulders, neck and back, while his heart beat and his breathing slow. It's a relief to strip off several damp layers of clothing, although they'll be necessary later on. Max bends to open the rucksack and to put the bundle away. He stops, motionless, as though in the grip of a giant invisible hand. Sweat and tears unite to blur his vision. He squeezes his eyes tight shut but fails to erase the image balanced on the stone in front of him: a small, green baby carrier.

He tries to blink it away, eyelids fluttering like feathers in the wind, but it doesn't help. Nature's soundscape is muted so that Max can hear only his blood pulsating in his ears. His skin turns ice-cold and alabaster white. Panic rises in him as his shaking hands grasp at his rucksack. Max struggles to stuff the clothes inside then manages to pull the thin cords to close the inner pocket. His legs can only just support him and the confused maelstrom that is his stomach makes him want to throw up.

He slumps onto the now empty rock seat and swallows several times, hoping to dislodge the dry, painful lump in his throat. Nausea subsides and he leans forwards, elbows pinned to knees, hands pressed to his forehead for support. He blanks out the world, drawing long deep breaths through his nose: cold air in, warm air out. *Come on*, he says to himself. *There's nothing to fear, no more surprises for you now.*

Max remains like this for several minutes, trying not to think about anything, just listening to his breathing. He lifts his head and watches his right index finger stroke the two patchwork hearts sewn onto the back pocket of the rucksack. Their softness comforts him. She had secretly made the hearts and attached them in readiness for their honeymoon in the Lake District. Such a beautiful gesture, one that made him fully realise the gift of feeling complete.

Until he'd met her, Max had never considered that love could be so powerful, so overwhelming. That it lay waiting to pounce upon and surprise him at any moment: slender fingertips pushing a stray hair away from her face; her uncontrollable laughter when he slipped over in mud; her quiet tears during a film; the delicious taste of her when they made love. Max had walked into an unexplored land where she welcomed him. The anticipation of seeing her never failed to excite every particle of his body, always filled him with happiness. She devoured all the possibilities that life offered and made him hungry for them too.

Sometimes, just before drifting into sleep, he would look at the outline of her body lying next to him in bed and try to imagine that space without her. When the thought became unbearable, Max would put his arm across her, drawing her warm softness into his body and burying his face in the richness of her long, black hair, the last of his tears left hanging on a few loose strands.

68

To fall in love is a dangerous pursuit if there is nothing in place to soften the fall. You pray that someone will catch you, embrace you, invite your heart into theirs. Max took that leap and the universe listened. When his son was born, the final jigsaw piece of Max's life was put in place. Not one of those boring straight-edged pieces of sky or grass or sea. No - the piece that is always difficult to find because it's fallen out of the box or rolled under a chair. The illusive piece that lies at the centre of the jigsaw, the picture inconceivable without it.

Panic retreats and a buried memory of the Fairy Throne from six summers ago unveils itself. A time before Max and his wife learned that their son was different from the other children in the nursery.

While they stopped for a rest, a beautiful Painted Lady fluttered down to land on the stone seat next to the baby carrier. The little boy's expression lit up with astonishment at the sight of the butterfly's metallic jewel-like appearance. Squeals of delight didn't disturb the fragile-winged creature. Nor did the perfect tiny arms as they waved and pointed, little creases appearing and disappearing at the elbows.

The ecstatic child didn't know what he was looking at but it demanded all his concentration. And Max witnessed the butterfly's beauty through the child's eyes, as though seeing it for the first time; a gift from son to father, experiencing afresh the details of a world that become invisible or lost with passing time. She made a butterfly mobile and suspended it above the cot. But it hung there, unobserved and forgotten, gathering dust until it was thrown away.

The sun ambles behind a solitary, stationary cloud hanging in the sky like a parachute. Cooling sweat on Max's shirt drives forces a shiver through his bones. He checks his phone again but still there's no signal. Nothing can penetrate the ancient layers of these monumental mountains, clad in swathes of thick heather and dense bracken, a light velvet-green moss grasping at any hard surface where it can find purchase. He zips up the phone in one of the rucksack's side pockets.

No phones; it's the one rule he insists upon during counselling sessions. Talking therapy doesn't work when it's disrupted by a jarring ring tone or an intrusive message notification. His clients need the freedom to articulate the negative thoughts and emotions that linger in a dark hallway, an old photograph, a chair, school, bedroom, relationship; the mental and physical sensations that manifest themselves in depression, anxiety, trauma, panic. Only then does the entrapment of hopelessness, the crushing weight of paralysing problems begin to find escape in the consulting room.

The furniture, objects and spaces in Max's office harbour a silenced chorus of human pain. At night, the anguished voices of despair lament their agony in the imprisoned darkness. They withdraw in the morning light, waiting for others to join them in due course. While empathetic, Max has always maintained a professional distance, never allowing himself to be drawn into the challenging worlds of his patients.

It is a dangerous no-man's land; he's witnessed a few colleagues crossing the line, becoming too involved, and returning with their permanent scars. So Max was well prepared to face the lows as well as the highs in his own life. Or so he thought.

The rucksack feels less burdensome as Max steps onto the path again. He turns his head, switching his gaze between the choice of continuing upwards or returning down to the car. Which one should he choose?

Why change his mind on such a beautiful midsummer's day and with so much daylight still to be enjoyed? Max finds his rhythm again. Two hours pass. Two hours of constant uphill through a landscape that seems to be retreating from Max as he fixes his eyes on the path. Heather, bilberry bushes, bracken, ferns, thistles, hare bells, gentians, campions, tormentils, bog myrtle, milkwort - they grab at his ankles and calves, catch in his socks, all vying for attention before vanishing. A gang of noisy crows mess around above a dark ridge while two stonechats, perched on a weathered gorse bush, conduct a heated conversation.

Max remains undistracted, glancing from the ground a few metres in front of him up to the distant summit which is now in view. But that isn't where he's heading today. He has another destination planned. With a strong sense of purpose Max leaves the path, stepping across knotted heather and wading through thigh-high reeds and bracken.

The undergrowth's sweet moisture occasionally flicks up to land on his face. It's the sort of vegetation where ticks gather to leap onto and feast upon hot-blooded humans. Max knows the serious health risks of Lyme disease associated with ticks and always checks for the nasty little hangers-on after a walk. Today he couldn't care less about them as he charges on.

The vegetation thins out and ends at a beach of fine white sand in front of a calm loch. Near the shoreline is an old wooden love seat with a swivel mechanism that enables its users to admire a 360 degrees panoramic view. Should anyone tire of staring at the loch they can turn to admire the northern hills, or the path approaching from the south, or the white-bladed wind turbines to the east.

Max puts his rucksack on the seat and sits down beside it. He and his silent companion look westwards across the loch and far beyond to the slim ribbon of sea. Max knows every word of the inscription that burns into his back as he leans against the weathered wood. He turns and his fingers search for the worn letters carved into the oak backrest.

Carry me over the water,
Leave me at the lochside,
There my love is waiting,
To greet me at eventide.

He traces the letters of '*my love*' over and over, gently pressing his fingertips into the darkened grooves. The words transfer to his lips and slowly repeat themselves as Max, almost hypnotised by his actions, shifts around to face the loch again. He spreads his arms wide across the top of the bench and tilts his head back to rest on the old wood. The lonely cloud has vanished and he stares into the blue emptiness above him.

Just over a year ago the empty void that now occupies his body was filled with love. Often it was a love that was tough and painful and unbearable. But sometimes it was joyous and uplifting and fulfilling and even surprising. Whatever kind of love it was, it meant that there were people who existed and mattered to him, that his life had purpose. But all of that was stolen, ripped away from him by the very person whom he trusted and loved more than anything else in the world.

Why, why, why? Thoughts, words, names create a chaotic and destructive scene in his mind. The turmoil is always agonizing whenever this question chooses to assault him to launch its unexpected attack on him. Shaking his head from side to side,

Max thumps his fists against the seat, desperate to fight off his dark demons that demand his attention. He jumps up from the bench and strides down to the shore. He knows he mustn't lose sight of why he's up here on this somnolent summer's day.

The loch exhibits a rare stillness today as its water absorbs the azure sky. There's not even a baby's breath of wind to disturb it. Max smiles as he watches a rainbow-decorated dragonfly flit along the water's edge, not daring to touch the surface and get its gossamer feet wet. A perfect reflection of two summits interrupted by a grassy saddle spreads across the mirrored surface; an inverted world where sky floats beneath land. Leaning his head down to one side, Max gazes at the enormous butterfly created by nature and its reflection.

He lifts his head up and stares across the water to a tiny white rowing boat on the distant shore and behind it a small woodland of birch and rowan. The loch's surface captures every detail in a perfect transcription. The scene's purity sweeps across the water towards Max, embracing him, one moment clinging to his body, the next, rushing through every fibre, every nerve, cleansing him, absolving him.

Such richness of beauty is too unbearable for Max and he shuts his eyes. But the image remains, gradually disintegrating into a watery kaleidoscope of fragments that push from beneath his long eyelashes and tumble down his face. Some of the tears bypass his convulsing body and drop to the sand, their shards of unequalled perfection soaking into the millions of tiny grains at Max's feet.

He's experienced this emotional ramraid many times during the last year. It still astounds and him and knocks him off-balance, like an unannounced updraft from a steep-sided cliff. Max waits for the surge of intense energy to subside before he opens his eyes. Then he picks up a small, flat stone from beneath his left boot and skims it across the water, watching it bounce three, four, five times before diving below the surface. The mirror doesn't shatter but melts in liquid ripples that spread out like giant fans, growing larger and larger.

He scans the ground for more stones, continuing to skim them across the water until baby waves start crawling over the pebbles towards the white boat on the opposite shore. After ten minutes, Max pauses, leaning forward to rest his hands on his thighs. His shoulders rise up and down in response to his heavy breathing while the water sways and dances in front of him. Exhaustion overcomes Max as his legs fold beneath him and he collapses to the ground.

It was the diagnosis that had shifted the axis of their world. Up until then they thought their son was just a late developer. According to all the reference books they had read, it wasn't unusual for boys to start talking later than expected. But for months and months he failed to make any sounds other than crying. And he didn't do much of that. He preferred to sit on his mother's lap at the weekly toddlers' group while his playmates ran and screamed and tumbled in an excited blur of energetic discovery.

'Mamma' and 'Dadda' tripped clumsily from his thin pale lips a few days after his second birthday. Some more words and phrases crept out and the relieved parents wondered what all the fuss had been about. Then they heard just two words, uttered by a specialist, which sent their lives spinning in unexpected directions. Muscular dystrophy.

A therapist and a life coach should both be well-placed and have the skills to deal with such a devastating situation. After all, they're trained to recognise other people's crises and help them come through, adjust, accept. And at first, Max and his wife coped quite well. They counselled their own feelings of grief, anger, and depression, able to recognise the text book indicators as they rose up in their minds.

Their son, meanwhile, was happy and coped with hospital visits, medications, machines. He knew no other way of living and displayed a resilience nourished by unconditional love. But an unyielding path of deterioration was the only direction he could take. He didn't have the recovery or improvement options that were available to many of his parents' clients.

His parents marked their child's milestones with giant leaps between delight and despair; his first words; his first stay in hospital; his first day at school; his first wheelchair; his first invitation to a party; his first day of home schooling; his first holiday; his first oxygen mask. When the difficulties started outweighing the glimpses of normality, his mother remained with him, watching her child's arms, legs, spine being twisted and deformed like an ancient olive tree. Watching him strain for breath with every tiny effort, his muscles wasting, his failing heart struggling to beat life into him. She was his constant companion.

It was exactly one year ago, on a Friday morning in June, that his wife killed their beautiful little boy and then killed herself. She crushed some sleeping tablets into his breakfast and while he slept, she smothered him with his favourite Peter Rabbit pillow. Afterwards she washed his frail body, her tears helping to bathe the cooling skin. The flannel traced the disfigured outline of his curved spine, his under-developed limbs, his tiny, fragile ribcage encasing the heart and lungs that would have eventually failed his spirit. When she finished, she dressed him in fresh pyjamas and put him to bed, stroking his soft, golden hair and kissing the pale forehead.

Max found them lying side by side when he returned from work that night. He was afraid to wake them as they looked so beautiful and peaceful. The physical pain and mental frustration of his son's existence was terrible to witness. Every working day, Max helped to mend people's broken minds yet he was unable to repair his boy's deteriorating little body.

When Max noticed the little plastic containers, emptied of his son's medication, blood began to pound through his veins as the unthinkable became the possible. He whispered, then spoke their names, and was soon shouting them, his hoarse, unanswered voice slipping through the narrow crack of the open sash window and escaping into the warm evening air.

Max took three quick paces into the room, his right foot kicking the empty malt whisky bottle which then rolled under the bed and settled next to a toy car. Uncontrollable screams of denial tore through his throat as he scrambled among the bedclothes searching for breath, for pulses, for any sign that that the most dreadful event had not occurred in this room. That this had not happened to his family.

His crazed mind managed to get a shaky message to his trembling fingers to dial for the emergency services on his mobile. His voice was controlled enough to provide sufficient details. Max knew he had to remain calm. There was still a chance. He tried mouth to mouth resuscitation, frantically alternating between mother and son, willing them to live. But there was no response from the cold blue lips as he kissed them over and over again. No warm sigh of breath, no movement from chests. He even tried lifting his wife's body to make her vomit the fatal cocktail she had consumed. Her dead weight was too much for him. Exhausted, he lay her back down on the bed.

Max stared and stared. Convulsions rose and gathered momentum as they strove to escape from inside him. He closed his tearless eyes, and as his head fell backwards, he opened his mouth, stretching his lips, his jaw, his cheeks into a silent scream. The silence was broken by a noise so dreadful, so primeval, like that of a wounded or dying animal, that Max didn't recognize it as his own. But he was beyond all recognition, all sense of what was happening around him. He was abandoned upon a tide of raw pain. He didn't hear the voice on the phone or the doorbell ringing, or the people forcing their way into his family home.

Max is woken up by the vocal ascent of a skylark. He's lying on his side and as he opens his eyes, he watches a tiny spider, about two inches from his nose, negotiating the pebbles as though they are an enormous boulder field. He doesn't know how long he's slept for. The left side of his face and neck are hot where they've been exposed to the direct sunlight. Max licks his dry, cracked lips as he stands and gets a drink from his water bottle. He doesn't have any food with him. His appetite left him along with everything else. He empties the rest of the bottle over his head, swearing as the cold attacks his hot scalp and bites at his skull.

Fully awake, Max chooses some large, jet-black stones and arranges them to spell out his name on the sand. They're about the same size as the ones he collected last year for the water feature he wanted to build in the garden. He takes his fleece jacket from the rucksack, puts it on and fills its pockets with more of the stones. Their colour and smoothness are so attractive that he decides to collect a few more in his rucksack.

Max smiles as he recalls how she'd cried out in pain that day she'd rolled off the rug and over some sharp shingle when they were making love on this beach. One of those precious hot days in the north when the wind had gone visiting elsewhere, taking all the clouds with it. A day with a stillness so rare you could hear the mountain's elements living and breathing: water, rock, earth, trees, plants, animals, insects, all dancing and rejoicing in the radiant energy of the sun.

Max remembers her smooth skin beneath his fingers and how she responded to his touch. He sees the curve of her body as she lay naked on her side facing away from him and looking out over the loch. He'd traced its outline, so like the peaks and corries of the land surrounding where they both lay. Then he'd gently massaged the discoloured imprints at the base of her spine. The rich scent of her body, mingled with the gentle aroma of her favourite perfume had slipped inside him like a genie returning to its lamp. All of Max's wishes were granted that day.

It's time to leave. Max picks up his rucksack then immediately drops it when the mobile phone in the side pocket judders to life with a text notification. He looks at the bag, then the sky, and then the bag again. Surely, it's not possible to get a signal here? Max pulls out the phone, passing it between his hands like a hot coal, as he tries to decide whether or not to read it.

He presses a button and stares motionless at the name of the sender. A lone cloud that has crept unnoticed across the sky now threatens the benevolent sunshine. He closes his eyes to keep back the tears that are threatening to overwhelm him again. *I can't speak to anyone right now*, thinks Max. *Especially not her.* He draws back his arm and hurls the phone in front of him. He follows the trajectory of its journey as it arches skywards before plunging into the water and unsettling the loch again. The ripples he creates seem to wave at him and he waves back.

Max heaves the rucksack onto his back for the last time and takes the first steps on his return journey; steps that will not return him to his car, his empty home, his workplace. His pace is slow and tentative at first, made all the more unsteady by the shocking cold around his ankles. A terrible weight in his heart almost anchors him to the unevenness beneath his feet. A weight as heavy and burdensome as the rucksack filled with rocks, its material stretched so much that the two patchwork hearts appear to have doubled in size.

Hot, wet tears burst through all the barriers and cascade down his creased face. He stumbles over rocks and stones, water filling his boots and sucking at his clothes as it rises up to claim him. The mobile phone that spiralled down to rest on the loch bed took with it the message from Max's sister.

R U coming 2 party 2morow? Birthday boy so looking forward to seeing his Uncle Max. Wants 2 go walking with U soon. Ring. Love U. XXX.

But Max is led onwards by a vision of two familiar figures on the opposite shore. They stand beside the white rowing boat and gesture at him to join them.

The floor of the loch banks steeply, allowing more water to crawl into pockets and empty spaces, to seep into clothing and hair. Max's breath is fast, faster than when he was walking uphill. His heart stamps out the warning inside his chest that he is in danger, while his brain screams at him to stop. But his will, his desire, his spirit, his soul, whatever this force is within him, drives him onwards with neither hesitation nor doubt.

He manages to call out their names just before the balance tips and he is dragged down into darkness. *They haven't heard me*, he thinks, and he thrashes his arms, desperate to break the surface one last time and to cry out their names.

The sun, having chased away the rogue cloud, relaxes in the sky. It's in no rush to go anywhere soon, especially today. The heat slows down the numerous walkers who have come to explore the mountain on midsummer's day. From high above, they look like inquisitive insects. They stop to greet each other and to wipe sweat from their eyes as they drink in the view. Some of them go no further than the loch. It is a beautiful destination – far better to appreciate it than climb to the summit in this temperature.

A couple enjoy tea and homemade cake on the love seat as they listen to the charged energy in the voices of their young children who have discovered a name spelled out with stones in the sand. Tiny pink hands grab one black stone after another and hurl them into the water. The splashes and ripples transport their excited screams to the opposite bank, setting the white rowing boat to a gentle rocking motion.

They descend to the crowded carpark as eventually do all the other visitors and by late evening one car remains. The living, breathing mountain locks away another of its secrets, shrouding it with the inhaled heat of the long day. Three swans idle in the shallows of the loch while the northern midsummer light refuses to fade away.

Where fortunes lie

'Hiya, Jean. It's only me. Sorry I'm a bit late.'

'I'm in the lounge, Barbara. Stick the kettle on while you're out there and come and help me with this computer.'

'I'll be right there.'

'And bring my tablets while you're at it. Kill two birds with one stone.'

Jean's been reading her Tarot cards while she's been waiting for Barbara to arrive. They seem very promising considering what she's got planned for this morning: The Wheel of Fortune for change, the Sun for success and Justice for fairness. Well, this is her interpretation, based loosely on what her mother had taught her as a child.

In all honesty, the readings have never come easily to her and she often constructs them to suit the situation. People expect the daughter of a soothsayer to have the same prophetic powers, that they must be passed on. But Jean is no Cassandra and, touch wood, no one else seems to have worked this out so far. Nor does she like to disappoint people or send them away with bad news.

Take Mrs. Riley's reading last week, for example. The Lovers, the Hermit and Death – passion, solitude and the end of something – were inappropriate cards for a 95-year-old with a pacemaker and a weak bladder. Thankfully, Mrs. Riley's eyesight is fading so she was happy with the Fool, the Chariot and Strength: optimism, progress and courage. Too happy and too visually challenged to notice the ladder she walked under on the way home. She'd died instantly after being hit on the head by the slate tiles that had slipped from the hands of the roofer. *Such a pity*, thinks Jean.

78

Barbara appears in the room with two mugs, a teapot, a milk carton, a bowl of sugar and a plate of biscuits on a tray. Her skin bears the grey, creased pallor of a woman who might smoke in her sleep.

'Took me a while getting out of the flat this morning.'

You still got your little problem, Barbara?'

Barbara stands still. 'What d'you mean?'

Jean's arthritic fingers gather up the ancient cards into two piles and she slowly crams them back into their tattered boxes.

'You know. The weird stuff with the front door.'

'I told you, Jean. They don't consider my repeated locking and unlocking of the front door to be a problem.'

'Well, it sounds like a bit of a problem to me,' says Jean, putting the cards away in a drawer. 'Especially if it makes you late.'

'It was much worse after the break in,' says Barbara. 'One morning, I was so panicky, I did the locks fifteen times.'

'But Barbara, doesn't that put you somewhere on the OCD septum?'

'Spectrum, Jean, and no it does not.' Barbara adjusts the tray so that the edges line up with those of the table.

'Oh well, fingers crossed you don't get there. Did you shut the backdoor? Don't want that bloody great black cat from number thirteen in here again. The mess he made...'

'Anyway, you can't be too careful about security in this neighbourhood. No, you're alright. I saw him nip into the bush under the window cleaner's ladder next door when I was coming up the garden path. A heck of a lot nicer now that you've gravelled over the crazy paving, Jean. Trying to dodge the cracks did my head in every time.'

Barbara puts the tray down so that its edges line up with those of the coffee table. The sleeves of the ill-fitting navy-blue carer's uniform concertina up her pale arms. A tarnished charm bracelet on her bony right wrist rattles against the dusty glass surface.

Jean notices Barbara's damp hair. 'Is it raining?'

'Third day in a row,' says Barbara, sitting down next to the laptop on the settee and removing a memory stick from her pocket.

'Well, I hope you haven't opened your umbrella to dry off in the kitchen again. I can't believe you did that and left your new shoes on the table.'

'They were a beautiful blue suede and the damp ruined them.' Barbara flicks open the memory stick and puts it into one of the laptop's USB sockets.

'Hardly surprising, with you bringing all that misfortune into my house,' says Jean.

'You and your superstitious nonsense, Jean.' Barbara switches on the laptop. 'You sure you don't want to check I haven't got 666 etched into my scalp?'

Jean chooses not to respond to her carer's stupid comments. If Barbara wasn't of some use helping her with this online stuff, she'd have made a complaint. But that can wait for the time being.

'Tell you what, Barbara, let's use my best china in the display cabinet. The tea set with the four-leaf clover pattern our Monica bought me for Christmas when she got that waitressing job in The Pot of Gold. Lovely pub – you been in there?'

Not waiting for a reply, Jean levers herself out of the armchair. Upright and stationary, she sways for a few moments like the inflatable Michelin man outside Hodgson's garage at the end of the road. She shuffles around the overheated room and returns with the cups and saucers. On the sofa, Barbara stares into the screen of the laptop now resting on her knees. There is a gunfire rattle of chipped nail varnish hitting the keys while her eyes, like two pinballs, ricochet around, chasing the instructions in front of her.

'Bingo!' she cries.

'I thought we were playing the Lucky Cat Slots like yesterday....'

'Yeah, we are, Jean, I've just found the site. Now, take your pills before you start.'

'...'cos I was so close to that jackpot yesterday and all good things come to her who waits.'

Barbara's over-plucked right eyebrow arches its back and the skin above her top lip puckers in a hairy ripple. She takes a deep breath into her oily lungs and hands the laptop to Jean.

'OK, Jean, take it steady now. You've loaded five hundred pounds on there, but with a few careful pulls, I reckon the Lucky Cat's gonna pay out today. D'you remember which keys to use?'

But Jean's already hitting her way to victory, her stiff, deformed fingers suddenly springing to life and searching out the caps lock, shift and arrow keys. Barbara pours them both some tea and pecks at a custard cream. Watching the old lady hunched over the keyboard, Barbara is surprised with the success of her latest client. Perhaps it's beginner's luck but who says you can't teach an old dog new tricks?

'How's your Geoff doing, Jean?'

Jean's varifocals are ablaze in a kaleidoscopic whirl of brilliant light. Periodically, a cacophony of bells, whistles and high-pitched cheers burst out of the laptop and fill the room.

'Come on, my beauty, here we go. In for a penny, in for a pound.'

'Geoff – how is he?' Barbara scratches her palms as she waits for Jean's reply. They've been itchy for a couple of days now and she wonders if she should change her washing powder. Had Jean noticed this, she would have told Barbara that she could expect money to be coming her way soon.

'I'll give you the full story in a minute, Barbara.' A thin, tinny trumpet fanfare proclaims a win on the digital one-armed bandit. Jean pauses for a few gulps of tepid tea and then resumes her quest.

Barbara smiles as she hears one of her favourite songs trickle into the room from the kitchen radio – Rose Royce singing, 'I'm wishing on a star.' *I certainly am*, she thinks.

Jean pauses, staring at the screen as she waits for the final round. 'Stitches are out and he's back on the minicabs.'

'He's like a cat with nine lives, your Geoff,' says Barbara, pouring herself some more tea and pocketing the rest of the biscuits for later. 'He's had so many accidents of one sort or another, I've lost count.'

Jean continues, ignoring Barbara's comment. 'Mind you,' says Jean.' he's a bit shaken by it all. Fancy that, not losing control of the car when it hit the black ice but then getting smacked in the face by those dangly rosary beads when they flew off the rearview mirror. The crucifix got him right across the bridge of his nose. Not a real Catholic, you see. Only signed up when he married Bernadette. Perhaps it was divine restitution.'

'Retribution, Jean.'

But Jean forgets Geoff and everything else as the view in front of her lights up and she's invited to play again. Her pulse shifts from canter to gallop as she reins in a few more wins and approaches the big one.

'Here we go, Barbara. Fingers crossed, this is it!'

You can cross all your toes and chuck a bucket of salt over your left shoulder, thinks Barbara, *but it's not going to help you, you stupid old woman.*

Suddenly the screen turns black, the sound effects are silent and bright yellow letters spell out, "LUCKY CAT WINS – TOP UP ACCOUNT TO CONTINUE." Barbara finishes her tea and looks at her watch. She's desperate to get out of the house for a smoke.

'What the hell happened there?' says Jean, picking up the laptop and shaking it. 'I haven't just gone and lost it all again, have I?'

'Not to worry,' says Barbara, putting all the tea things on the tray to take them into the kitchen. 'You're bound to win it all back tomorrow. Just like last time.'

Jean sinks back into the settee cushions. 'Couldn't you set it up for one more go?' she says in a childlike voice.

Barbara stands and looks down on Jean. 'Now you know the rules. 'Fifteen minutes each day, otherwise you might become addicted and then where will we be?'

'I know, I know,' says Jean, folding her arms and squashing her spare chins onto her chest. 'I just hate leaving the game when I'm losing.'

'But you've got the luck of the gods,' says Barbara, as she walks across the room. 'You're far too clever to be parted with your money.'

'I suppose. Tell you what, pick us up some fruit scones and a pint of milk tomorrow and we'll have a little celebration. My purse is in the bread bin.'

Barbara looks at Jean with an empty smile. She knows exactly where the purse is. It's one of the first things she locates in a client's house.

Jean realises she must have nodded off when she's woken by Barbara shouting to her from the kitchen.

'I've left your lunch out ready to pop in the microwave.'

'Thanks,' mumbles Jean, who has completely lost her appetite.

'See you tomorrow. I know that jackpot is just around the corner. I can feel it in my bones.'

Panic suddenly rises in the old woman's voice. 'Remember to leave by the front door. Can't have you coming and going out the back. It'd bring worse luck than the mirror falling off the bathroom wall last weekend.'

As she leaves the house, Barbara throws a dismissive glance towards the horse-shoe that was nailed above the porch on Jean's wedding day, nearly fifty years ago. She makes a call on her mobile, carefully planting her feet in the middle of each paving slab as she walks up the road.

'Charlie, did you get it all? And when will it be in the account? Tomorrow? That's smashing. Nah, the old witch didn't suspect a thing. Thinks tomorrow's her big day. Life savings? There won't be any life left in her after the medication she's been on. I'll get us a bottle of bubbly on my way home. The first of many, eh? Get packing, love.'

Now Barbara is dying for a cigarette. Placing one between her lips, her thumb pulls on the catch of the silver-plated rabbit foot lighter Charlie bought for her birthday. She tries a couple of times but it fails to ignite. Everything would have been fine if only she hadn't at that moment stepped on the pavement stone crack and run hysterically into the road. And so, her luck ran out, just as it had done for the rabbit. The driver of the number seven bus swore that she came out from nowhere.

Moira Harris

Inheritance

Tom rattles the poker in the large wrought iron grate, enticing the slumbering flames to stand up and resume their dance. Replacing the elegant brass object on its stand, Tom turns to reflect upon city life beyond the drawing room window. His contemplation is interrupted by the approach of a drunken argument that pauses on the pavement below. The shrapnel of exchanges pierces the orange glow of streetlights, flying up like fireworks and exploding in front of him.

'You promised me....'

'Yeah, in a minute, just give us a light...'

'I bet you bought her chips...'

'Look, I told you...'

'You gonna see her now, then?'

'Look, just shut up, OK?'

The battle of words moves onwards, dying beneath a meandering click of high heels. The fashionable street is silent once more. Tom stares at the full moon pinned to its thick, black sky like a piece of child's artwork. Tonight, it casts an enormous white cloak across the desirable Victorian mansions, revealing rows of sleek cars parked on forecourts. Palatial homes and gardens built for the rich, now extended and divided into smaller dwellings with tarmac lawns for the richer.

Tom imagines his employees on this cold, clear Friday night performing their ritual stagger from pub to bar to club. The moonlight guides them along their path towards the pursuit of excitement, of adventure. Strong spirits consumed, leading to high spirits and then low spirits. At the evening's climax they are all the very best of friends, valiant and invincible blood brothers. In the graveyard hours they will stare into the abyss of their empty souls reflected in an unfamiliar and grubby bathroom mirror.

Tom set out on the same destructive path when he was very young. He followed it for many years, finally choosing to change direction before it was too late. He drank to cope with both the drunken abuse dealt to him by his father and the agony of losing his broken mother. He toasted the death of his brutal 'Pa' with magnums of champagne, praying for the existence of Heaven and Hell. Despite all this, Tom became successful: a lucrative asset management company, beautiful wife, owner of several homes, all the rewards that wealth delivers.

He stopped drinking just before reaching the age when his father's liver had ceased to function. Tom didn't want to become his father's son, lying in the gutter with the ghost of that abhorrent man. Conquering his addiction was a struggle but now Tom is the victor: healthy living, rejecting the faith that couldn't protect his mother, donating a sizeable proportion of his fortune to charities, delegating business decisions to those he can trust. Life is simpler yet richer than anything his money can buy.

The apartment door opens and slams shut. Tom returns to his fireside armchair and the collection of short stories he is reading. After a few minutes, the tall, blonde, designer-clad figure of Estelle enters the room. The firelight's reflection shimmers in a large glass of red wine loosely held in her right hand. She leans against the door frame to steady herself. Tom turns a page and waits for her to begin.

'Where's the pipe and slippers?'

Tom glances up at his wife's smirking, Burgundy-stained lips. He returns to his book then speaks.

'Hello Estelle. I thought you'd be in the country this weekend.'

'Party at the Hodgson's. You should have come. Oh, I forgot. Not your sort of thing these days. So why are you here?'

'Actually, it's the opening of the new respite centre at the clinic tomorrow.'

'Of course. Saint Thomas of the Hopeless at work again.'

Tom adjusts his glasses, trying to concentrate on the words in front of him. 'We're both invited, you know.'

'Can't. Weekend house party. The Hodgson's new place on the coast. Awfully sorry.'

She gulps down the last of her red wine.

'Well, try not to embarrass yourself too much, Estelle.'

'God, I preferred you drunk,' says Estelle, stumbling towards the kitchen. 'Now, you're just so bloody self-righteous and boring.'

While his wife opens another bottle, Tom closes the book and stares into the hot, red embers of distant childhood evenings. His father, drinking away the housekeeping every Friday night then falling through the door with his inebriated demands. His poor mother, always trying to stay one step ahead, always trying to please. The foundations of his formative years laid down in a bed of painful and wicked unpredictability. But he's come so far and won't be dragged into this territory again. He will have complete control. Tom takes several deep breaths then stands to rake over the dwindling ashes of the fire.

He hears Estelle's mobile phone ringing in the kitchen. She answers, her inaudible words punctuated with a playful laughter that Tom knows too well and cannot ignore. He studies his face reflected in the mirror above the mantelpiece. After a few minutes, Estelle shouts through to him.

'The Hodgson's are picking me up early so I'm going to bed.'

'Goodnight, Estelle.'

Tom remains motionless for a while, listening to the dying breath of the fire. He leaves the room, the moonlight catching a flash of the brass poker gripped in his hand.

Moira Harris

On holiday

'Any drinks or snacks from the bar, sir?

The words wake Andrew with a shudder from his dream in which his plane is moments away from crashing into the sparkling sapphire sea. He looks up at the face of a middle-aged woman, her hair dragged back into a painful-looking bun. A vertical tide mark in front of her right ear is the dividing line between cheap foundation make-up and a glimpse of pale skin. She leans against the metal trolley and her blue uniform buttons battle to contain a roll of fat which conceals a long-forgotten waist. Staring at her wide, gloss-lipped smile and huge unblinking eyes, Andrew is reminded of a blow-up doll.

'What? Erm, yes, I'll, ermm…. whiskey, no ice, please.'

Andrew's racing heart slows to a steadier pace. His gaze drifts in an arc, stopping abruptly at the glaring face of Colin.

'And I'll have a gin and tonic with ice,' says Colin. 'If it's not too much trouble.'

'And a gin and tonic.'

The stewardess doesn't hear Andrew's second order above the internal drone of the aircraft. She continues to prepare his drink and calculate the cost.

Andrew clears his throat. 'And a gin and tonic please.'

'What's that you want, sir?'

'A gin and tonic please.'

'With ice,' hisses Colin.

'Ice and lemon, sir?

Andrew looks from Colin to the stewardess who are both now staring at him. 'Just ice, please,' he says.

89

She hands them their drinks along with a pile of paper napkins and several white plastic stirrers. Colin pours the tonic from its miniature bottle into the clear plastic tumbler packed with ice. He stirs his drink. Andrew pays and then holds up his tumbler to examine its meagre contents. A couple of ice cubes float around in it but he hasn't the heart to summon the woman again to change his order.

'God, they charge the earth, and I bet it's some cheap blend.'

'That's never stopped you before.'

'Hm.' Andrew swallows a large mouthful of the burning golden liquid. Colin fiddles with his purple Kindle.

'You were snoring again.'

Andrew wipes his mouth with a napkin. 'Was I?'

'Yes, you were. Really loudly. It's so embarrassing. You're getting worse.'

'I had a terrible nightmare about the plane crashing in the sea.'

'You'll have a worse one if you fall asleep again before we reach Lanzarote.'

Several hours later, Andrew is seated by the pool of the exclusive four-star Hotel Casa del Embajador. Colin is resting in their room. The early start, then delays at Heathrow had made Colin tetchy all day. He needs a break, thinks Andrew as he finishes eating a plate of meaty black olives and sips his whiskey. He shifts his chair to get the last of the day's sun and feels a sudden twinge in his lower back. Colin always insists that they push the twin beds together and the ones in this hotel are made of heavy mahogany. Andrew is always reluctant to do this. He can't bear to think what the room staff might think, as if any of them actually care.

Some of the guests relax on elegant recliners beneath large, deep blue umbrellas emblazoned with the hotel's imperial logo. Andrew traces the steady progress of a hazelnut brown man's rhythmic breast stroke in the pool. A woman with a sculpted physique poured into a white bikini waves at the passing swimmer. Andrew glances down at the pale marbled legs emerging from his own three-quarter length linen shorts and sighs. His turquoise polo shirt fails to conceal a broadening girth.

They've been coming to Lanzarote in March for as long as they can remember, always staying in the same resort. That was until last year when a friend recommended this fantastic new hotel in

Playa Blanca. Their rejuvenating and enjoyable stay at the Hotel Embajador had impressed them so much that they knew they had to return here.

Andrew is delighted that it's not one of those unofficially gay establishments. He appreciates being surrounded by people like himself, nearing retirement and comfortably off. And the added bonus of no children thrashing about in the pool or killing the atmosphere in the restaurant with their demanding screams.

They didn't bother Colin. He'd always wanted a family but the idea of adoption way back in those early years had been out of the question. Andrew was always thankful for this as he'd never warmed to the possibility of parenthood.

Colin appears at the edge of the terrace, pausing beneath an archway overflowing with bright red geraniums and creamy-white honeysuckle flowers. Andrew watches him scanning the pool area and smiles, unable to contain a sudden surge of pride. Colin's base tan, acquired at great expense in a London salon, offsets the distinguished cut of his silver hair. His neat, upright figure is clothed in a slim-fitting purple and white striped shirt, tailored white trousers and Italian leather shoes. Andrew uses this moment of uncertainty in Colin to admire his partner of thirty years. He looks as gorgeous now as when they first knew each other.

'Now I'm ready for my holiday,' says Colin, sliding his new Ray Bans up to the crown of his head as he joins Andrew at the small marble table. The waiter arrives with the large gin and tonic Andrew has requested for when his companion appears. Colin thanks the sallow-skinned young man with an appreciative smile.

'You're looking great, Colin,' says Andrew. 'Even better than the day I met you.'

'The heat's got to you already, I can see. Or maybe that's the whiskey.'

'Nonsense. You sang *Nessun Dorma*, remember?'

'Of course, I do.'

Andrew takes a folded white handkerchief from his pocket and wipes the sweat from his forehead. 'But can you remember where you sang it?

'In a room full of drunken philistine lawyers who weren't listening.'

'I was. And I was looking too.'

Colin leans across and places his hand on Andrew's arm. 'How fortunate there was one opera-loving legal bore hanging around that evening.'

Andrew grins at Colin then finishes his drink, the fading pink ribbon of sunset reflected in the bottom of the glass. Colin's manicured fingers swipe the screen of his iPhone.

'Come on, Col, I'm famished. The fish menu looks fantastic.'

Colin's eyes flit across the text on the screen. 'Thought I'd just check the singers have all arrived in Berlin. It's an important gig tomorrow.'

Andrew stands and removes his jacket from the back of his chair. 'We agreed. No work this holiday.'

'But there might be a ...'

'Look, the company has been touring for years and there's never been a problem. Not with Mad Margaret in charge.'

One last swipe and Colin puts the phone away. 'Where would I be without you?' he asks.

'Probably chatting to that gorgeous young waiter behind the bar. Now come on. I've got us a table overlooking the sea.'

They soon settle into their holiday routine. Rising early, Colin runs along the beach and then heads to the health suite for a punishing gym workout. Andrew enjoys a cooked breakfast on the terrace and then strolls along the landscaped esplanade. He stops for coffee, checks his emails and has a few brief telephone conversations with clients.

They meet up for brunch at a vegan café Colin discovered last year. Colin is ravenous and tries to persuade Andrew to have something a little bit more adventurous than a green salad. Then it's back to the hotel's private beach or poolside where they position themselves in the shade of straw-covered parasols. Andrew's fair skin easily burns so Colin fusses over him with suntan oil and a large hat. The sun, however, worships Colin, coating his body with a delicious honey hue. They return to the tranquillity of their suite in the late afternoon where they rest from the heat or make love. Then it's aperitifs at the hotel bar followed by a stroll into town for dinner at one of the exclusive seafront restaurants.

One evening, in the middle of the week, they are in their favourite restaurant, the *Casa Roja*, waiting for their main courses to arrive.

Andrew admires the large boats rocking to and fro in the marina below.

'Yacht or cruiser – which would you prefer, Colin?'

'Hm?'

'We should buy a boat when we retire. Sail around the coast.'

Colin pours them both another glass of the Rioja Reserva he selected from the wine list.

'Everything alright, Col? You're quiet this evening.'

Yes, yes, I'm fine. A bit drained by the sun and exercise, I expect.'

'Well, don't overdo it, OK? This is supposed to be a holiday, remember.'

'At my age, this body is high maintenance, darling.'

'Don't be ridiculous. You look great. Anyway, I thought we might take a cruise around the other islands tomorrow. I was speaking to that German couple we met on the first...'

'I want to get married, Andrew.'

'To me?'

'Of course, to you. Don't make a joke of it.'

Their food arrives and a few minutes pass in silence while the waiter arranges everything. Meanwhile, Andrew finishes his wine and refills his glass. Colin stares through the window at the blackness of the night sea. The waiter establishes that there is nothing else they require and leaves the couple to enjoy their meal.

Andrew picks up his knife and fork and puts them down again. 'We've already discussed this, Colin. You know how I feel.'

Colin pushes a piece of squid around on his plate.

'I know, darling. But I can't get it out of my mind. It's something I really want to do. Want us to do.'

'But why, after all this time? Surely that civil partnership nonsense was enough?'

'You know that made sense. Now I want to be married to you. I just want what everyone else has.'

Andrew gestures for another bottle of wine.

'I think you just want to show off to all your theatrical friends with a big party. I don't mind that. Let's do it but without the fiasco of a big gay wedding, OK?'

'Do you honestly think I'm that shallow?'

'I'm sorry, I was being facetious.'

Andrew bites his tongue as he chews his filet steak. His glowering red face resembles one of the buoys floating in the marina.

Colin dabs the corners of his mouth with a white linen napkin and tries again.

'So much has changed, Andrew. And we should change too. Before it's too late.'

Andrew continues eating, staring down at the meal he had so been looking forward and trying to ignore the pain in his mouth.

'We need to consider our age. If something happened to one of...'

'So, is it money you're worried about, Colin?' You'll be a wealthy individual when I pop my clogs. Better watch out for the gold diggers.'

A few heads turn in their direction.

'Keep your voice down, Andrew. You know that's not what I'm...'

'Well, for God's sake, isn't thirty years a big enough sign of my commitment to you?'

'I'd rather have a wedding than a bloody boat. And I can look after myself. You're not the only successful man sitting at this table, you know.'

The argument disappears into a wordless vacuum. Andrew summons the waiter who is very concerned that the gentlemen have not finished their food. Unable to tempt them with anything else on the menu, the waiter goes away and returns with the bill.

'I'll get this,' snaps Colin, as Andrew finishes the second bottle of wine.

The following morning, Andrew is woken by the maid coming in to the room to change the beds. He has sufficient Spanish to ask her to return later on. Then he reads the note Colin has left on his bedside table.

'We both need some time alone today. See you at the hotel bar at 6.00. Colin.'

Andrew feels as though one of the island's iconic volcanoes is erupting inside his skull. He scrambles around in the bathroom looking for the headache and indigestion tablets that Colin has packed in his toilet bag. He washes the tablets down with a bottle of still water from the minibar and takes a reviving shower. He gets dressed and heads towards the lighthouse.

The weather is cooler today and most of the visitors have deserted the beach for cafes and sheltered resort pools. Andrew is grateful for the westerly breeze that helps clear his head. As he walks barefoot along the water's edge, the repetitive ebb and flow sucks and blows life in and out of the smooth, golden sand beneath his feet.

Andrew recognizes that his behaviour last night in the restaurant was unforgiveable. His arguments were pathetic, considering he constructs them so well when he appears in court. He knows he doesn't have a case against Colin because Colin, as always, is so right. They have loved and supported each other far longer than many heterosexual couples they know, so why not celebrate this amazing achievement with marriage?

But Andrew always puts up obstacles whenever the subject arises. He's scared of the next step. Scared it will change things, that it will change Colin. He'll want more than Andrew can offer: someone younger, more exciting, unpredictable, adventurous. Andrew just wants things to remain as they are.

***

After an extra vigorous morning workout, Colin feels the need to immerse himself in something cultural. He takes a taxi to a museum he's read about and spends the afternoon wandering around an exhibition of work by Spanish art students. The museum is the former studio home of the artist, Cesar Manrique, a native of Lanzarote whose work was influenced by the natural beauty of his native island. Colin can't understand why he hasn't visited it before.

He enjoys viewing all the paintings and sculptures which have been inspired by different objects washed up on the beach. He is also amazed to discover that Manrique was an important advisor and instigator in the preservation and sensitive development of the island as it is today. *We've fallen in love with Lanzarote because it is a work of art*, thinks Colin.

Two hours of absorbed viewing leaves Colin both elated and exhausted as he enters the museum's cafe. He treats himself to a cortado and devours a generous slice of chocolate cake served to him by a young waitress with a beautiful smile. As he eats, he's sorry that Andrew isn't with him. But he's also annoyed with his partner for being so pig-headed about getting married.

Colin knows Andrew didn't mean any of the things he said last night. He's lived with him long enough to recognize when the defences are going up. He loves Andrew and the life they share together. If only he could persuade Andrew that gay marriage is neither a spectacle nor a freak show. It's their entitlement to show each other and everyone else just how important their love is.

Colin doesn't want the concerns of this rambling dispute to ruin his afternoon. He looks around the empty café and tries to translate some of the renowned artist's quotes which have been carved into the walls. The longest one above a large picture window defeats him.

'It is so lovely, yes?'

Colin turns and sees the waitress standing behind him, looking up at the elegant script.

'I'm afraid my Spanish isn't very good,' he says.

'I will translate for you.'

The melodic lilt of her clear voice settles the words inside Colin's head.

'For me, it is the most beautiful place on earth and I realise that if they were capable of seeing the island through my eyes, then they would think like me. Since then, I made it a point to show Lanzarote to the world.'

A surprising heat of emotion overwhelms Colin. His heart thumps fast and loud and he can't contain the tears that blur the words above him. A noisy family burst
s into the café and the waitress returns to her place. Colin leaves a large tip and runs out into the late afternoon to find a taxi.

***

Andrew reaches the headland marked by the slim, white lighthouse. He stops to wipe the sweat from his eyes, cursing himself for forgetting his hat and a bottle of water. The breeze has disappeared, allowing the sun to heat the island once more. There are no cafes this far out from the resorts but Andrew is determined to get to the very end of the path.

Continuing onwards, he hears a gentle burble of voices. It grows louder as he approaches two Spanish fishermen seated in deckchairs. One is thin and bald and wears flowery Bermuda shorts. The other has his long grey hair in a pony-tail. Seeing their exposed skin, Andrew is reminded of the dark leather sofas in the

Hotel Embajador's evening lounge. The animated exchange is now at full volume. Several empty beer bottles float in the melted ice water of a battered cool box while the lines from two well secured fishing rods descend to the motionless sea below.

One of the men breaks away from the conversation and turns his smiling, wrinkled face to greet Andrew. As Andrew returns the gesture and nods, he notices the words printed in English on the man's black T-shirt: 'I love my wife.' *Someone in his family obviously has a sense of humour*, thinks Andrew. He can't help but wonder why life is so uncomplicated for some people and not for others. Standing at the end of the path and staring out to the horizon, Andrew is uncertain how he'll face Colin later on.

There is a sudden shout from one of the Spaniards. Andrew turns to see a large, silvery fish being reeled in by the old man in the T-shirt. His arthritic companion excitedly offers advice while somehow keeping his pipe clenched between gapped teeth. Andrew smiles at the thought of some poor woman gutting the catch later on, just as she has done on many occasions over the years.

He remains seated on some rocks until the fishermen begin to pack up at the end of their day. Andrew knows too that he can no longer delay his return. He stands and nearly falls into the sea as T-shirt man plants a kiss on his companion's cheek and they set off before him, holding hands.

***

At quarter past six, Colin asks the young waiter for another gin and tonic.

'Hey, Colin, what do you think?'

Colin turns and looks in amazement at Andrew who is standing behind him, wearing a strange, T-shirt and holding a large fish. Sweat pours off Andrew's red face as he hands the prize catch to the startled barman.

'Tell chef to do something special with this for dinner.'

'Andrew, have you been…'

'And we'll have a bottle of champagne right away.'

'Andrew, where on earth did you….'

'Colin, I hope you still want to marry me because tonight we're celebrating our engagement!'

Moira Harris

The branch is broken

If the dog hadn't reappeared this morning, Carolyn wouldn't be listening to the echoes of her pain fading into the high cobwebbed corners of the kitchen.

'Damn, damn, damn.' *Fuck, shit, bollocks.*

It's happened again. Steadying herself against the sink, she tries to turn on the cold water tap. At first it won't move in either direction because someone has been over-zealous in turning it off. If only that someone would replace the broken washer then the tap wouldn't need to be screwed tight shut to stop it dripping.

Her good left hand grabs a tea towel with an enormous red heart design printed on it. She wraps it around the tap, giving her better purchase. As the swaddled silver tap yields, she watches the cold water pour down onto her stinging right hand. The screaming copper kettle whose boiling hot handle she'd grabbed a few minutes ago now sits in accused silence on the stove.

Carolyn can't believe she's been stupid enough to scald herself again. It must be the third time this month. She'd rather have an electric kettle but the wretched thing had been a family Christmas present when the new kitchen and Aga had been installed. No one had considered how heavy and impractical the kettle was even if it did look impressive.

The soothing rush of water relieves the pulsating pain in her tender finger tips. Some of its coolness trickles inside the arm of the large navy-blue towelling dressing gown and collects in a little pool at the elbow before soaking into the material. When her hand is almost numb and the pain begins to subside, Carolyn turns off the tap and wipes her fingers dry on the grubby cuffs turned over twice at the wrists.

The action disturbs a faint aroma of teenage aftershave embedded in the material. A glimmer of recognition briefly skips across her face then vanishes. But the glimmer has delivered her with a memory, the type that leaves her entire body frozen other than the tears that fill her eyes. Carolyn knows she must blink them away; knows she must find a distraction before becoming overwhelmed.

The row of plants on the windowsill needs some attention. One of them, the white orchid, a gift from her next-door neighbour, is dead. A solitary flower lies in a dried, shrivelled bundle on top of the crumbly compost. Two faded green leaves curl upwards like the hands of a beggar asking the question, 'Why?' The stake that had once supported the delicate plant now leans in a state of solitary redundancy. Three blood red geraniums in chipped terracotta pots are still fighting to stay alive. Carolyn takes a dirty glass from the sink and fills it with cold water for the plants. One after the other, she watches the liquid gather on the parched soil before it seeks a path among the surface cracks and runs away.

Looking through the window she sees the large black dog underneath the rowan tree at the bottom of the garden. The animal digs relentlessly around the roots, preparing a space to hide away its secrets. Carolyn bangs on the glass but the animal ignores her.

'Why don't you just bloody well clear off?'

She'd like to open the kitchen door, to run into the garden and scare the animal away. But she can't. She's afraid to cross the threshold, afraid of what she might discover.

Carolyn quickly swivels around to face into the kitchen. The chimes of the grandfather clock in the hallway announce that it's lunchtime but she's not hungry. She knows she should eat well; she's been told often enough by so many people. But it's so difficult without much of an appetite for food. For anything.

Even the lingering smell of burnt toast hovering in the grey light has no effect. She's become accustomed to this souvenir from her daughter's abandoned breakfast. Every morning, Carolyn listens to the familiar sounds of Sally rushing to get ready for school. She never sees her daughter at this hour. It's too early for Carolyn these days and she prefers the sanctuary beneath her duvet. A muffled exchange of words between father and daughter in the kitchen swims around Carolyn's pillow. Then the little Swiss cowbell hanging on the backdoor knob is transformed into a claxon as Sally slams her way into the day and an early team training run.

The high-pitched whine of the smoke alarm fractures the echoes of this departure. Carolyn doesn't care. She knows her husband will be cursing as he flaps yesterday's newspaper around to disperse the smoke.

There was a time when Carolyn would have gladly died in her burning house. But she's been administered to with methods, ways of changing her thoughts replacing them with new ideas and outlooks. A recent development is that Sally has stopped crying during the night and Carolyn is pleased for her daughter. She's jealous of her too.

Carolyn dampens the heart-embossed tea towel, using it to pick up the kettle like a weapon at a crime scene. She makes a mug of strong black coffee and clears a space for it in the sea of papers, crumbs and general paraphernalia that permanently reside on the oak kitchen table. An embossed, scalloped-edged card slips from one of the dusty piles and drops onto the sticky tiled floor. Carolyn picks it up and holds it at arm's length to read the inscription printed in waves of golden italics.

"Like branches on a tree, we may grow in different directions but our roots remain as one."

She draws breath like a deep draught of energy, screws up the card and throws it into the recycling box. It nestles among a forest of forgotten news.

The oblong parcel delivered early that morning sits beacon-like on the empty fruit bowl. She moves to open it but instead her hand reaches far down into one of the cavernous dressing gown pockets. Fizzing fingers gently play with the familiar small plastic bottle, the pink and white capsules tumbling like Chinese acrobats inside. They were supposed to keep the black dog away. But he was at her bedside in the early hours, the reflection of dark hopelessness festering in the deep green pools of his eyes.

Carolyn's hand releases the unopened bottle as she slumps down into her chair. Her head rolls forward to rest on her chin, heavy eyelids shutting out an undesirable world. The tent of electric light above her head illuminates roots that haven't seen a hairdresser for months. How will she get through another day? Yesterday was bearable but today she can taste the sour flavours of her mood. Even the liquid genie in the vodka bottle hidden in the utility room won't be capable of washing them away. She struggles to comprehend Peter's ability to carry on, how he manages the pain.

'Because I have to, darling. We've got to pull together, if not for ourselves, then at least for Sally. She needs us to be strong, to be there for her. She really needs you, Carolyn.'

'But I wasn't there for Jake, was I? I missed all the signs. His own mother and I couldn't …'

A rattling shudder rampages upwards from the base of her stomach and grips her throat hard as the hot, fat, tears spill from her eyes. Peter knows her words by heart, each one a concrete slab in the sinuous path towards the inevitable argument. This morning he stepped off the path, avoided the cracks, took a different route.

Now, opening her eyes, she stares at the blurred backdoor, imagining his distorted silhouette beyond the frosted glass shrinking to a tiny dot where he departed hours ago. Blinking away some of the sorrow, Carolyn's gaze is drawn to the scuffed linoleum below the row of coats hanging by the door. There is so much activity gathered in the regimented line of shoes: running, cycling, tennis, rugby, hockey.

None of the shoes belong to Carolyn. She prefers the role of the spectator, shouting encouragement from the crowd while standing in her fleece-lined pink wellies. Preferred the role. The spaghetti jumble of laces ignites an image of plump little fingers learning the knots and bows; intense concentration scrawled on newly-creased foreheads, tongues poking through rosebud lips. The shoes are arranged in groups of three different sizes, patiently waiting for Goldilocks to come and try them on.

A pair of blue cross-country shoes returns her stare. Two cold gaping black holes that haven't felt the warmth of feet for nearly a year. The dexterity of an invisible hand folds Carolyn up like a piece of origami and pushes her across the floor on her hands and knees. Confused, she sits with her back against the dishwasher door, hugging her knees to her chest with the running shoes cradled in between. Terrified eyes scan the room from behind the veil of her fringe as she desperately tries to reclaim yet another fragment of passing time hewn from her existence.

On Monday mornings, after a weekend of family sporting events, the kitchen was particularly pungent.

'Jake, how many times do I have to tell you to rinse those shoes under the outside tap before you bring them in here?'

Lowering her head now, Carolyn can only detect the detergent she has used to try and clean away the memory. She wants to pull her body inside her to stop the film that is about to play in her head. As the reels start turning, she watches herself and Peter at the finish line, cheering with the other parents as they get a glimpse of the front runners. Jake is easily leading by three or four metres. Her beautiful, tall, long-limbed, golden-haired boy. The image of his father and grandfather striding towards them. His pale body is blotch-red cold and muddy. His face is the same, but with the expectation of victory shining brightly in his blue eyes and his wide, determined grin. Arms held high, Jake is an enormous Y as he breaks the tape and earns the title of Senior Cross Country Counties Champion.

The crowd roars and Carolyn wills the film to stop here because she knows the final scene. But it won't stop. It never stops.

She doesn't want to watch Jake coming towards her with his sweaty running vest hug already prepared.

She doesn't want to see his ecstatic face suddenly distorted in agony as he crumples to the floor like the old industrial chimney they had all watched being dynamited next to the canal two years ago.

But it's all there, projected on the backs of her eyelids in full 3D technicolour with quadrophonic surround sound. She's by Jake's side with water but she can't rouse him from unconsciousness. Now his skin is translucent, the dirt on his face a map of the world sketched on pale tissue paper. Jake's coach is down on the grass opposite her, anxiously checking for breathing and a pulse.

Mouth-to-mouth resuscitation hasn't made any difference by the time the paramedics arrive. The ambulance swallows her sleeping boy amid a tangle of masks, tubes and blankets. She wants to kiss his blue lips which now match the colour of the running shoes discarded on the grass beside her. The film ends but there are no credits.

In the family room at the hospital, the pale young doctor told them that Jake's heart muscle had become too thick to pump blood. Sally pressed her wet face against her father's jacket, his arms instinctively containing his daughter's uncontrollable spasms.

Carolyn stared numbly at the green shoots of three hyacinth bulbs emerging from the bright yellow planter on the coffee table. The doctor's voice bounced off the walls of the echo chamber in her head. Their son, gone, while they, his parents, stood there, life coursing through them. Such a cruel re-ordering.

How could a young, fit athlete die of heart failure? Was it genetic? Was Sally at risk? The doctor, at the end of his ten-hour shift, took the time to explain that twelve young people die suddenly from undiagnosed heart conditions every week. Inexplicably, it was more common in young athletes. Outwardly he was extremely professional, trying to answer their searching questions with compassion. Inside, he simply wished he could repair the damage, the same wish he made day after day.

The gunshot crack of a car backfiring in the street startles Carolyn into the present. She returns Jake's shoes to their place in the line-up and hauls her stiff limbs up from the floor to her chair again.

A wafer of yellow sunlight breaks through the January dishwater clouds and lands on a shiny pamphlet. The diluted warmth illuminates three letters: CRY. Cardiac Risk in the Young. The charity was extremely supportive from the very beginning but now she wants her crying to stop.

As she sips her tepid coffee, Carolyn reads again about raising money for life-saving Automated External Defibrillators for schools and sports clubs. A year ago, she'd never heard of the amazing device that can shock the heart to restart its beat. Now she is told she can make a difference.

Carolyn switches her attention back to the parcel addressed to her, removing the white plastic wrapping and lifting the box lid. Despite knowing what's inside, her fingers shake as they part the white tissue paper to reveal a new pair of blue running shoes, size six. She puts on the shoes, leaving the laces undone for the moment. Her restored hand reaches for a pen and five minutes later, the entry form for the charity run is complete.

Carolyn walks across to the kitchen window, her eyes searching around the garden. The branches of the rowan tree gently wave at her, some of them seemingly pointing to the base of the trunk. Looking down, she sees the clumps of delicate snowdrops circling around its roots. Behind the tree, the black dog pushes through a gap in the hedge and is gone.

Moira Harris

It helps to be flexible

It really is a very simple task. Just to sit. Absolutely still. No need to think or speak or do. But she has a tiny spasm on the left-hand side of her upper lip. A miniscule muscle that nudges at her left nostril. And now she wants to sniff which may encourage a sneeze. And for some absurd reason sneezing has recently befriended her bladder so that all she can think about is peeing.

She needs a distraction. Miriam opens her bleary right eye. It blinks, eyelashes fluttering like a moth's wing freeing itself of morning dew. Her swimming vision struggles to find something else to focus on other than the psychedelic patterns that have been swirling around on the black screens behind her eyelids. She remains very still - a seated statue - fearing any movement that may disturb her environment. The tiny muscles of her open eye, a jade green search light, let her scan the view bounded by her peripheral vision.

The ocular wateriness settles as do all the other bodily urges that have tormented her up until this moment. Miriam strains her eye upwards to look at the large rectangle of sky suspended like an inverted Mediterranean swimming pool; the kind advertised in glossy Sunday newspaper magazines.

A large white seagull floats on the azure canvas of her upside-down world. The morning light is so clear that Miriam notices the bird's legs stowed beneath its bright white body. She can't see any of the other Velux windows in the cathedral-vaulted ceiling. There are other windows in two of the walls but they're positioned so high that it's impossible to see out of them to the world beyond. A prison had come to mind when Miriam first saw the building. Not what the architect had intended, she was sure.

107

Miriam relaxes her eye downwards, keeping her head still as her vision ambles anti-clockwise. Eleven pairs of eyelids sit with her in a wide circle. The eleven faces they occupy are all familiar, particularly the one to her immediate left. She can't see it right now because her nose is blocking her view. Miriam inspects the faces she can see, surprised at how different they looked when they entered the circle. There is the thin, nervous lady opposite her, recently widowed and wearing a magnificent amber stone ring on the middle finger of her left hand. Miriam can't remember the woman's name but notices her calm expression. They'd spoken briefly over an unidentifiable green smoothie cleansing drink at the meet and greet session.

'Hello, I'm Miriam'.

'Oh, yes, right, well, hello, nice to meet you, Miriam. We're... our name is... I mean, my name is...'

The woman had smiled too much when she spoke or was spoken to and rattled through everything she said as though her opinions had been regarded uninteresting and not worth inviting for years. But right now, she conveys nothing except empowerment and serenity.

As she continues her survey, Miriam notices the quietening of facial tics and twitches, the disappearance of crows' feet and laughter lines, and the recent arrival of a thin dark moustache on the upper lip of another woman who is staying in the room next to her. *Probably too exhausted to wax it this week*, thinks Miriam. Perhaps she should suggest the threading method; she's certain it would last longer.

Miriam always has her eyebrows threaded and her hair cut and styled every six weeks. She knows that hair and eyebrows frame the face and should never be neglected. The last time she visited The Hair Bare Salon in her local shopping centre, her favourite beautician was on maternity leave. Instead, she'd been assigned to The Ripper, a heavy set south-east Asian woman who entwined the delicate cotton thread around her muscular fingers and tore the hairs from Miriam's forehead. Miriam had been considering seeking help with her wiry chin hairs but decided to continue with her own scissors and tweezers for the time being. Even with a pre-med double shot Americano, she wasn't sure her pain threshold was a match for The Ripper.

Miriam's circumnavigation is halted by another eye staring back at her from the ten o'clock position. She smiles at her fellow cyclops squashing her left cheek upwards, concertina-like into her closed eye. The recipient of Miriam's lopsided grin, a thin, bald, bronzed man with a tiny diamond stud earring and a goatee beard, returns her smile. She notes two rows of perfect white teeth like bleached marble tombstones – could they be false or does he have an over enthusiastic dental hygienist? His silvery blue eye widens as the pink tip of his agile tongue, like that of a lizard's, traces the outline of thin lips. Miriam clamps her eye shut, attempting to erase the lascivious image and regain the inner calm she's supposed to be nurturing.

Unfortunately, her return to the pursuit for personal serendipity is blocked by a paralyzing cramp that overpowers her facial muscles. Miriam daren't open her eyes again for fear of engaging any of the circle with her circus clown grimace. And she certainly doesn't want the instructor, Elektra, to see her like this.

Miriam's stomach somersaults as she recalls the preliminary session earlier that week. She was the last of the group to introduce herself, injecting some humour after listening to so many earnest life stories and philosophies. Miriam's announcement that her abdominal muscles had disappeared somewhere over the Bermuda Triangle twenty years ago and that a slug of Campari in her morning green tea really sharpened her mind had been received in ice-cold silence. Now, long painful seconds subside and so does her face as it relaxes like the forgotten balloon that deflates in the high dark corner of a room days after the party is over.

The week-long retreat of meditation, mindfulness and yoga had been her daughter's idea. Rachel told her mother it would be the perfect opportunity to spend some quality time together while cleansing body, mind and spirit. All their holidays - a fortnight in length and devised and organized by Miriam - always started with the very best of intentions: healthy eating, cultural sightseeing, lots of reading, early nights, some gentle exercise and limited use of electronic devices.

They never learned that such high levels of perfectionism were beyond them and inevitably, the scales tipped, usually at the beginning of the second week. Food and alcohol consumption as well as general slothfulness would rise at the same rate as regard for holistic well-being and entente cordial would plummet. But these days it was difficult to find dates that suited Rachel.

Miriam had suggested spending the May half term week in Tuscany. They could enjoy each other's company in sunny and idyllic surroundings and return home before wanting to kill each other. One of Miriam's friends had offered her the use of a holiday villa in exchange for some A-level English coaching for a rugby-obsessed son. Miriam dreamed of days relaxing by the private pool, touring vineyards while tasting delicious Tuscan wines, visiting small village churches to admire the Medieval frescoes, sampling regional food, drinking rich smooth espressos in local bars while people watching and cycling along cypress-lined country lanes.

Meanwhile, Rachel had heard about this amazing spiritual centre in West Sussex which she believed would be beneficially nourishing for both of them. Since splitting from her latest boyfriend, Rachel had embarked upon a mission of self-fulfilment, self-worth and self-purpose. A quest for unlimited creativity, drive and motivation. An opportunity to make the choices that aligned with her values and would lead her to the life she desired.

Consequently, she walked away from her accountancy firm and was now the business partner in a vegan cafe-and-developing-world-markets venture. Rachel is neither a creative nor a cook but she contributes the other essential ingredients necessary for such an enterprise and manages to keep the whole questionable project afloat. Her partner, Noa, is a highly skilled raw food chef and very adept with both spiralizer and blender but hasn't an ounce of business sense.

Not wanting to disappoint her daughter, Miriam had agreed to the retreat, realizing Rachel had little interest in northern Italy's truffle oil, wild boar ragout, local speciality tripe or vintage grappa. She was happy to pay for it in the hope that Rachel might find a suitable soulmate in this environment. Miriam's generosity almost led to heart failure when she discovered the cost. They could have flown business class to Florence, used taxis all week and eaten out at excellent restaurants every night for the same price. She might be the well-paid head of the English Department at one of the country's top grammar schools but Miriam still expected value for money.

The meditation sessions start at 6.00am every morning. There is no clock nor anything else for that matter hanging on the clean white walls. Watches are forbidden but Miriam is sure they've been sitting here for at least half an hour. She always has her first strong coffee of the day at 6.30 and is now craving caffeine like a hardened user. She tries to distract herself by listening for the sound of Rachel's breathing next to her. It's very quiet but Miriam recognises it. When Rachel was a baby, Miriam used to gently open the door of the bedroom she shared with her daughter, listening for the audible reassurance of young life. She'd slept so well both then and as a toddler; such a bonus with no one else to help Miriam during all those nights.

It seems peculiar to Miriam that the memories of those early years have idled in her head this week. Most of them have remained submerged and unrecalled for years. In this present moment, she's supposed to be focusing on inhaling through her right elbow and exhaling through her left knee. But whenever Miriam closes her eyes, the image of Rachel's father keeps appearing.

According to the all-knowing Elektra, Miriam should be using her third eye, located somewhere on her forehead, to perceive enlightenment beyond ordinary sight. Miriam considers it to be a ridiculous notion. She's just so surprised and rather suspicious that everyone else appears to have one.

In the absence of her third eye, Miriam's thoughts drift back to the formative years of her teaching career. The inner London comprehensive was a tough arena in which to teach English Language and Literature but she worked out how to earn the respect and trust of the students and even started to produce some impressive results.

Evenings and weekends were filled with marking and lesson preparations but every Sunday morning she would leave her one-bedroom flat and take a bus into the city to walk in the Royal Parks. On the corner of Kensington Gardens there was an art deco café, The Oriel, which served real coffee and freshly baked pastries. Here she met Alfredo, an Italian waiter with broken English, a charming smile and an ambition to become an actor.

'English rose, I buy you drink, yes?'

Miriam paid for the drink and for several others when he was able to join her on her side of the bar. They had a few dates, always ending up in his 'piccolo' bedsit when his shift ended after Sunday lunch. Alfredo introduced her to Italian food which he prepared and which they ate in bed.

Of course, that wasn't all they did in bed, and Alfredo was happy to demonstrate other skills while endeavouring and failing to improve his conversational English. The sex was fantastic but it wasn't enough for Miriam and so she stopped visiting the café.

When she returned there six weeks later to tell Alfredo that she was pregnant, he'd returned to Italy. As an only child and with her parents running a bed and breakfast on Orkney funded by her dad's redundancy pay, Miriam was on her own. She managed six months on maternity leave and then returned to work, leaving Rachel in the capable hands of Edna.

Edna was a mother of four grown up children and provided childcare for several working mums on the estate. She was a mother hen, always with a line of duckling toddlers trailing behind her when she went out. Edna loved babies so she was delighted to have little Rachel in her care.

Even after twenty-eight years, the embers of Miriam's guilt haven't quite been extinguished nor the jealousy that used to flare up when the young Rachel cried out for her 'Auntie Edda.' Miriam has never admitted to Rachel that she was a baby conceived and born out of lust. On the contrary, Rachel knows that she and her mother were abandoned by a self-centred, resting Italian actor whom Miriam had once loved very much.

Miriam discards the photo-fit image assembled in her head: an older, greyer, wrinkled Alfredo, still waiting on customers in a forgotten village café in southern Italy. It's replaced by the snapshot of the radiant blue morning sky and she wishes the meditation group was outside on the wooden veranda. They'd had a session there on Tuesday but the sun sidled behind a slate-grey cloud, ignoring the arduous salutations it was being offered.

Unlike Elektra's lithesome figure, the timetables at The Spirit of Intention are inflexible, irrespective of weather conditions. Today's spiritual focus is a favourite place near water that each person finds relaxing and enriching. Miriam isn't sure her Friday evening bubble bath accompanied by a glass of chilled prosecco qualifies.

She's reminded of holidays when she was a little girl. Her parents always went to the seaside to take her away from city life. But Miriam hated the cold salty water that stung her eyes, and the sand that lodged in her hair, her sandwiches, and her knickers. Consequently, she and Rachel never had beach summer holidays until the petulant teenager demanded one because that's what all her school friends were doing. Miriam joined the pack of British parents sweating beneath large parasols on the Greek coast, all suffering the effects of cheap retsina, while young friendships were forged and broken in the surf.

Miriam searches for another watery image but now all she can think about is going for a pee again. It would all be so much easier if the she wasn't being tormented inside this featureless box by the hint of a rare, warm, dry English summer's day.

Someone starts to snore. It sounds like the same person every day. No one dares take a look to see who it is. There isn't even a snigger, a stifled laugh, an awkward cough. Miriam was bursting to share the joke with Rachel when it first happened.

'Oh, come on, Rachel, how can you take this all so seriously? It wasn't you, was it?'

'No, Mum, it wasn't. And if you were a bit more mindful then perhaps you wouldn't find it all so amusing,'

As the gently mouthed 'ssshhh' develops into its familiar throaty purr, Miriam is tempted to have another peep but can't bear the thought of engaging with the grey goatee again. She doesn't think it's him. His neck's far too skinny. Thick-necked people, often men, are the culprits. She'd read about it in The Sunday Observer.

Miriam visualizes the handful of suspects in an identity parade. Most of them are the women in the circle, not including Rachel or herself. She wouldn't be surprised if it's the same person who farts without shame or apology in the evening yoga session. Problems at both ends of the gut.

That's something else she'd read about. The snore climaxes with an enormous grunting inhalation through the nose, followed by silence as if the perpetrator has suddenly died. A few seconds later life resumes with a stammering release of breath on the letter 'f' like a desperate attempt to say the word 'finished.'

'Finish now, please finish now.'

This is Miriam's chosen mantra today and it reverberates like a silent echo in every part of her body. Her dry mouth is jasmine flavoured, as though she's chewed the incense sticks which are lit and relit by Elektra. The mandatory glass of warm lemon water at 5.30am would taste much better with a few ginger biscuits.

Now she is tortured by the smell of grilled bacon, a cruel olfactory hallucination when breakfast will be a wheatgrass shot and a system boosting smoothie packed with avocado, kale, broccoli, beetroot leaves, whey powder and goodness knows what else. A broad palette of greens has saturated everything consumed so far this week. Rachel spends every meal time trying to convert her mother to the cause.

'It's because green foods are rich in vitamins, proteins and anti-inflammatory nutrients and it builds a strong immune system. At your age you should take this stuff seriously, Mum.'

'But I haven't yet reached the age nor the incapacity where I need everything mashed down like baby food, Rachel. Kermit the Frog committing suicide in a blender is not my idea of breakfast.'

'Who?'

Her radar picks up a muffled conversation drifting in from the garden through the one window that's been opened slightly. Something else to distract her from the need to pee and to break the unbearable silence. As an exam invigilator, she often wants to scream or laugh or sing during the three muted hours. Thankfully, the rustle of a turned page or someone putting a hand up prevents her from acting on her instincts. At home, the background noise of the radio is always broadcast throughout the house. Shouting at invisible politicians and experts is the norm.

Miriam wishes she hadn't chosen a cross-legged position this morning. Her hips and knees feel like rusty old hinges. She recalls how strenuous last night's yoga class had been. Thankfully, Elektra had encouraged everyone to move extremely slowly out of a seated position before lying down. Miriam had thought it was a miraculous achievement to move at all.

Each participant had, in total silence – talking is forbidden in all sessions – settled into the corpse position. Miriam hates this description. It's like poking a big stick in the Grim Reaper's ribs and inviting him to help himself. *If I die now*, she'd mused, *I'll be in the perfect position for a coffin to be constructed around me*. She was even wearing heavenly angelic white. Which would be all well and good if she had an ounce of religious belief in her.

After three days of yoga, Miriam is no stranger to perfecting her not-quite-dead-yet corpse. She focuses on her breath, cold air entering her nostrils, warm air departing. She is aware of the rise and fall of her abdomen and of her body sinking further into the bleached wood floor with every exhalation. If nothing else, she's sure the effect of gravity must draw the skin of her sagging cheeks and puffy eyes down towards her ears and take at least twenty years off her.

'Lawnmower' and 'hot' are the only two words Miriam can recognise before the disappointing exchange outside drifts away. She's fed up with her useless mantra which is refusing to manifest itself. Her mind requires another diversion.

Miriam considers how she's spent the best part of three days with her fellow spiritual seekers of enlightenment and yet she knows so little about them. The Spirit of Intention doesn't appear to include social interaction in classes as one of its objectives. Even during meals, when there is the opportunity to talk, no one seems particularly impressed by or even interested in hearing about her educational work. Rachel, however, seems to know what to say and has become quite popular within the group.

'Vegan suppers.' Miriam threw the two words into the dinner table chatter one evening like a couple of hand grenades. 'Really, what are they?'

The voices trailed away and Rachel leant back in her chair and looked at the ceiling.

Miriam poked at the contents of her bamboo dinner bowl. 'I expected energy enriching food combinations but can someone please tell me how this is going to improve my gut?'

The grey goatee started to speak. 'I think you'll find that your microbiome will...'

Miriam wasn't listening. She called over a staff member and ordered bread for everyone so as to make their cold raw soup more palatable.

'I'm afraid that's not possible,' said the young man, revealing two rows of braces on his teeth as he smiled at her.

Rachel saw the fire of indignation being stoked in her mother's eyes and stepped in to prevent the situation escalating to catatonic levels.

'Mum, everything is gluten free on this course and bread of any kind isn't included.'

At this point the young man should have walked away but youthful innocence compelled him to bestow some kind of conciliatory compromise. 'I can offer you our homemade vegan pumpernickel bread?'

Miriam was ready this time. 'You can certainly offer it,' she said, looking straight at him, 'whereupon I can offer it to the compost bin and leave out the middle woman.'

The young man, still smiling, backed away from the table. Everyone except Miriam and Rachel returned to their food in silence.

'Honestly, Mum, can you just eat your dinner.'

'Well, I'm happy to buy some bread, if that's what it takes,' said Miriam. 'Look, that lady over there has got two wholemeal rolls.'

'Yeah, but I think she's doing quilting.'

Miriam pushed the bowl away. 'Lucky her.'

Miriam is convinced that some of the course members must have secret supplies of forbidden food in their rooms which they fall upon and devour when they scurry away from classes. She wishes she'd had the same idea, although she's surprised that they weren't all searched for illegal chocolate and alcohol on arrival. Mealtimes are so subdued. It's just not what Miriam is used to. She teaches young women to be intelligent, confident communicators, for goodness's sake.

One afternoon she tried to engage with a lady while they were on a mindfulness walk and out of sight of Elektra. Miriam discovered that her name was Angela and that she lived in Swindon. But that was all.

'I'm sorry, Miriam but we're supposed to be walking ten metres apart and in a long line within view of each other. I'm afraid I can't chat and be mindful.'

Miriam got the message and dropped to the back of the party to admire the beautiful sea campion and thrift. It was when she emerged from an area thick with the coconut aroma of bright yellow gorse that she realized she'd lost sight of the others. After much tramping of paths Miriam hadn't a clue as to her whereabouts. She couldn't phone Rachel or anyone else because mobile phones were prohibited from mindfulness walks. As were all personal belongings including money and credit cards.

Fortunately, Miriam wandered into a small hamlet where the occupant of an attractive Tudor house, on hearing of her predicament, invited her inside to use the telephone. Miriam called her PA.

'But Miriam, why do you need Rachel's mobile number? Isn't she with you?'

Miriam, too embarrassed to explain her current plight, mumbled something about leaving her phone at the retreat and wanting to ask Rachel to book a table at a lovely rustic restaurant she'd found on a stroll around Hastings.

After a few more pleasantries and aware that her Good Samaritan was wondering if he'd done the right thing allowing this woman into his home, Miriam put the phone down and picked it up again to call her daughter. As she heard the ringing tone switch to voicemail, she remembered Rachel didn't have her phone with her either.

'Hi, love. If you get this, I'm in the village of Lower Minton. Perhaps you could come and get me? Hope you're being more mindful than me.'

Miriam knew her message was pointless. She told Arthur – she was on first name terms with the houseowner by now - the name of the retreat. He'd never heard of it. Then she remembered the name of a pub the group had walked past earlier; it had stuck in her mind because she thought they'd all be much better off in there having a chat over a ploughman's and a decent beer.

The Snooty Fox was about two miles away, according to Arthur. He was quite relieved to wave goodbye to this peculiar woman when he dropped her off there in his car. Miriam was just thinking what a shame it was that she didn't have any money for a cool, crisp sauvignon blanc when she heard the exasperated shout.

'Mum! Where the hell have you been?' Rachel, sweaty and red-faced, was marching across the grass towards her. 'We've been looking everywhere for you! Elektra is on the verge of a nervous breakdown and about to call the police.'

Miriam realized then that she needed to up her mindfulness skills to survive the week and ensure that her daughter didn't disown her.

The deep tones of Elektra's voice drag Miriam's thoughts away from chilled white wine and back to the meditation session.

'And so, we will conclude with three rounds of the Om mantra, awakening our bodies to receive the gift of the day that lies before us.'

Miriam has forgotten about the embarrassing chant and battens down the loud groan that is threatening to burst from her throat. She'd like to adjust her position but fears her knees will snap if she attempts to uncross and cross them again. She tries to get

Rachel's attention with a small cough but her daughter is already waiting to begin, her eyes closed, her body still. This is always an awkward moment as no one knows when to start of finish the sound. Miriam considers opting out but she doesn't want to disappoint Rachel or get another one those 'I know and see all' looks from Elektra at the end of the session.

Elektra begins and the others join her. 'Ooooooooohhhhhhhh...'

The door to the room bursts open.

'Oh, I'm very sorry. I'm looking for Beginners' Pottery.'

'mmmmmmmmmmmm.......'

The chant fades to a whimper as the circle's inner eye turns its vision outwards towards the intruder.

'No pottery wheels here, sir,' says Elektra. 'The wheel of life is all that concerns us.'

Maybe for you, but some of us have more far-reaching wheels to keep turning, thinks Miriam. At the doorway stands a tall, dark-haired man in his sixties, dressed in jeans and wearing a checked shirt beneath his blue linen jacket. He's surprised that The Spirit of Intention caters for religious sects.

'Right, yes, well, any idea where I can find the right room?'

'You'll need to ask at Reception.'

'But I've just come from there.'

'And there you must return, sir, if you're going to throw any pots today.'

'I do believe our guru's ruffled,' Miriam whispers in Rachel's ear.

'Are you concentrating, Mum?'

The gentleman nods awkwardly and retreats from the room, making three shuddering attempts to finally close the ill-fitting door. Miriam manages to contain the laughter inside her as they all listen to the footsteps diminishing along the long wooden corridor.

Tranquillity envelopes the room once more.

'Let your eyelids gently cover your eyes and remember to breathe naturally.'

Elektra's voice makes Miriam want to hyperventilate just for the hell of it.

'And let us recommence.'

There is a pause followed by a communal inhalation. During this moment, a line of words, arrow-like, fires through the window from the garden and pierces everyone's spiritual aura.

'For fuck's sake, George. You've forgotten to put petrol in the bloody mower again.'
Miriam snorts. The class ends.

Moira Harris

Belated

Babies have a little knowledge of the world before they are born which is why some are keener than others to enter it. The twins, for example, learned something about their special gifts from the muffled conversations that were interwoven with the background music. Fragments of phrases danced around them as though a volume switch was being erratically turned up and then down. They discovered that their special gifts would soon emerge. They discovered that other family members had received these gifts and that it would soon be time to pass them on. But then a loud section of a Mozart concerto or a Beethoven symphony would interrupt the voices and the identity of the special gifts remained undiscovered.

He blocked out the dreadful noise by practicing his back flips and forward tumbles and kicking hard with his legs. This made the voices very excited. Then he mastered placing his perfectly formed fingers into nearly-finished ears when Birtwistle or Schöenberg burst in.

She, however, simply floated around, a tight bundle, eyelids closed in contemplation, a crescent mouth of pleasure splashed across her face.

The midwife grinned triumphantly when his wriggling limbs eventually beat at the air. His strong lungs screamed to turn the bloody music off. His sister pushed him from behind, screaming at him to hurry up and to shut up.

The house was full of music. He couldn't escape from listening to the piano and violin being practiced for hours every day. If he was in the same room, he would sob fat, wet tears, so disturbing was

121

the sound to him. To be gathered up and comforted by the player as the notes drifted and died above him was a blessed relief.

At bed-time the confusing arrangement of stars and animals suspended above the twins' heads was switched on. As it rotated, monotonously tinkling nursery rhymes described horrific accidents involving mice and spiders, people falling off walls or down hills and heads being chopped off. He cried out in his sleep as he drowned in a sea of terrifying nightmares.

She enjoyed all of it, gurgling, laughing and rocking to the simple melodies and their hypnotic rhythms as they led her along a slumbering path. When the grown-ups went out in the evenings, Nanny switched all the noises off and read quietly in her room. He eventually slipped and settled among the silent black waves of the night.

When the twins were three years old, the grown-ups decided it was time to begin unwrapping the special gifts. They sat him on the piano stool and he stared at the big, black wooden monster with its wide snarling mouth of sharp, black and white teeth.

'Play, play', they said, as they pointed at the pages of the shiny new music book and pressed his podgy pink fingers on the keys. But after a few long minutes he fidgeted and kicked and ran out of the room, into the garden. Was this really the special gift he'd been waiting for? He circled round and round the lawn, as the baby melodies she played with both hands floated among the cherry blossoms above his head.

The grown-ups helped him make a toy violin by substituting an empty cereal packet stuffed with newspaper for the instrument's body and attaching a ruler as the neck. 'Try to hold it under your chin', they said, as they contorted his left arm and twisted his hand around so that his fingers grabbed the thin piece of wood protruding from the box. But he defiantly threw his head back and the pretence dropped to the floor.

In the afternoon, he watched Nanny set light to it before they launched it on the duckpond in the park like a Viking longboat. It startled the moorhens before it vanished and slid down to its watery grave beneath the reeds and lily pads.

Every instrument that he refused was embraced by his sister with skill and accomplishment. In the classroom she was an academic shooting star while his butterfly mind fluttered and looped over facts and figures and thoughts, never alighting anywhere for very long.

At the end of every school year, she returned home, her trunk bursting with prizes and impeccable reports, he with a mountain of detention notes and angry red ink scratched across his prep work books. His greatest trophies, the playground battle scars of fights lost and won, were an embarrassment to the grown-ups as they struggled with the emotional volley of delight and disappointment.

He signed up for the swimming team trials because they clashed with choir practice. Until then, he'd stood in the back row every week with the mute baritones, those who'd been told to mouth the words and not utter a note.

She, of course, got all the solos and her high, sweet voice drifted across the hall like a lyrical rainbow bridge. Hopelessly messing around in the pool couldn't be any worse than imitating a goldfish rehearsing The Messiah, he'd thought.

The swimming coach eyed the troublemaker suspiciously as he jumped into the pool. He'd often seen the boy waiting outside the Headmaster's study or skulking into the detention class. But in the water the young unsettled mind discovered a peaceful rhythm and the strong thrashing body a sleek purposefulness. The astonished coach observed the transformation. His gaze fixed upon the figure gliding smoothly and effortlessly up and down the lane. Judgement switched like a turning tide and the boy finally slotted into the world.

Every spare moment was used for training, repeatedly cutting through the water, perfecting his technique, getting faster and faster. He loved to plunge into its warm blue opaqueness, exiting a world of noisy chaos and confusion and entering one of silent clarity.

His talent recognized, he swiftly moved through local and national events to represent his country at international level. He swam not for victory and medals but to feel alive in an environment where he was truly himself. The family didn't understand and didn't approve of such a ridiculous activity but he didn't care. Every stroke carried him further away from their narrow outlooks and loveless expectations.

Nanny kept in touch with her letters and congratulations cards. She rarely mentioned his sister nor his twin nieces who were now in her care and whose precocious temperaments she battled with daily in the arena of life. His correspondence wasn't as frequent but Nanny didn't mind. She knew that self-expression didn't flow easily from him.

Then one evening, when the grown-ups were out and the unruly children had finally gone to sleep, she sat by her fire to enjoy his latest letter. The envelope was surprisingly fat but when she read its contents she understood why. While his life had become busy with success, he was struggling to manage the practicalities of the world he inhabited. He needed her help and she knew she would willingly provide it.

The grown-ups were speechless when Nanny packed her bags in her car the next morning and drove off without any explanation. They had plenty to say when they read the letter that she had left for them on the piano. Her place was with her favourite boy and she wasn't going to offer them the opportunity of spoiling the situation by telling them her plans. He was delighted to offer her the comfortable life she deserved and an escape from his family. She was delighted to be able to look after him.

They travelled everywhere together, she cheering from the poolside and becoming something of a celebrity in her own right. They appeared together at charity functions and awards ceremonies where she was often mistaken for his proud mother. He never felt it necessary to correct this.

Her birthday was the one day of the year when he did not swim, neither for training nor for competition. Instead, they walked along the cliffs, pointing out tiny sailboats and soaring seabirds. In the evening she opened her present, a huge pile of books written by her favourite authors. He slept smiling on the sofa, undisturbed by the crackling fire and the contented sound of pages being turned.

Life in the raw

EAT FOOD THAT CAN ROT – EAT WHAT YOUR GRANNY ATE – EAT FOOD YOU CAN PRONOUNCE – PLANTS ARE BEST – NOURISH YOURSELF – EAT REAL FOOD

Molly doesn't need to read the mantras of magnetic and typed letters scaling the fridge door. The words they form were hammered into her memory a long time ago. She's even stopped adjusting the older ones that have a tendency to migrate south.

Today is Monday. Liquid raw day. She opens the door and removes her breakfast ingredients: wheatgrass, dandelion leaves, beetroot leaves, raspberries, avocado. She places these in the industrial-sized juicer with some purified water and a few drops of organic lemon juice and switches on the machine. It devours the contents with a deep- throated growl. She pours the transformed contents into a glass, watching the thick, dark elixir oozing like blood from a wound.

Molly drinks her breakfast at record-breaking speed and uses a long-handled spoon to scrape out the glass and not waste any of the expensive ingredients. Her recipe advises slow sips but even after all this time, the taste and smell still make her want to throw up.

It is five years since Jack was diagnosed with prostate cancer. He'd been complaining of back and hip pain but he thought that was just the after effects of a hilly marathon they had both participated in. It worsened, which led him to the GP and later to the life-threatening discovery.

Molly just couldn't understand why this was happening to Jack. They had what would be regarded as a healthy lifestyle – no fried or processed foods and always low-fat and reduced sugar. Jack enjoyed the occasional pint of beer or a glass of wine at weekends while Molly's memories of an alcoholic father kept her in check. They worked in a sedentary environment so time was always set aside for exercise.

She'd felt cheated. The disease had laughed at their adherence to the rules. Their life had crumbled like the chalky cliffs that pierced the sky above their favourite beach run.

Molly cleans all the parts of the blender, reassembles it and then turns her attention to a letter lying on the kitchen table. She had typed and printed it yesterday evening, deciding to leave it overnight before taking any further action. Molly reads it through once more, and satisfied with the contents, signs and places it in the waiting envelope. *It's time to send this*, she thinks, as she writes the address.

So much disturbing news had been delivered to Jack throughout his illness, both by post and in person. Sometimes it was positive and their world would expand by a hair's breadth. When setbacks arrived, Molly felt her body deflate, yet Jack always remained hopeful. She'd struggled to contain her fear, watching him endure invasive and painful treatment. They even thought he'd been the one to rip up the rule book, until the disease found a new home in his bones.

The kitchen clock tells Molly that she would be late for work were it not her day off from her marketing executive role with the large pharmaceuticals company in town. It's become the biggest employer in the area since she and Jack began working there twenty-five years ago. Her boss had been very understanding when Jack became ill. Time off for consultant appointments, treatment and surgery was never a problem, especially for one of their leading researchers.

When Jack took early retirement and his health became unpredictable, Molly had started working from home. She knew the powerful drugs had some terrible side effects but she believed in them. For most of her working life she'd pored over statistical reports and success rates to help promote these miracle cures.

Molly checks the contents of the vegetable box. She wants to be sure she has enough ingredients for a lunch-time smoothie and tonight's cold meal. Even after all this time, she's never thought of reverting to her old eating habits, something she could so easily do these days.

Turning over a shiny bell pepper in her hand she recalls the argument she'd had with Jack following his big announcement.

'So, after all we've been through, you're just going to give up the fight, are you?' Even now she can remember the fear and confusion rushing through her entire body.

'I'm only giving up those poisonous drugs.'

'Oh, so our work is the cause of all this, is it?'

'Don't forget that I'm the one who's enduring a living hell, Molly. I just want to be in control again.'

'You're insane. You'll be dead within a month.'

The following day she'd calmed down enough for Jack to describe the research he'd been doing. Bewildered, Molly listened to his theory of how raw, plant-based foods which haven't been stripped of their nutrients through processing, peeling or cooking can greatly improve the immune system. The body's healthy cells become rich in energy and fuel while the cancer cells are starved of the toxins and man-made rubbish they love to feed on.

'This must have taken you ages to put together,' she said, when Jack fell silent. 'Why did you keep it a secret? I could have helped you.'

Jack looked at his folder of notes and material, smoothing it with his hand. 'I suppose I wanted to be the one to ask all the questions, find the answers.'

'And you're absolutely certain about this?' She'd placed her hand over his, feeling the delicate bones through tissue-paper skin. 'You know what will happen if it doesn't work?'

'It's my choice, Molly. But I need you to do this with me.'

She knew there was nothing to be gained by opposing Jack. Nor did she have the right to do so. It was his choice, perhaps some corporeal instinct rejecting the drugs and guiding him towards an alternative path. How could she challenge him?

Molly packed away her doubts, sensing they would materialise in the future, and agreed to participate in her husband's unorthodox project. He would soon die and she didn't want their remaining time together to be consumed by anger and resentment. That would come later.

After a month of juicing, blending and munching through piles of chopped, sliced or julienned fruit and vegetables, Molly broke down and demanded two cooked meals per week. Jack investigated this and found that food cooked at a temperature of no more than 50°C complied with his method. She agreed to this luke-warm compromise, provided she could add fish and a few dairy products to her meals. At night, she fell asleep and dreamed of filet steaks and chocolate cake.

The low stock of fruit and vegetables prompts Molly to jot down a few items on her shopping list. How different it looks from the days before cancer: organic fruit and vegetables, nuts, seeds, pulses and a few of Jack's favoured green powders. The conservatory is awash with enzyme-rich sprouting trays brimming with wheatgrass, alfalfa, mung beans and broccoli. Jars of home-produced kimchi and sauerkraut sit on shelves and bubble away at various stages of fermentation.

She used to worry about the neighbours getting the wrong idea and had to explain to them exactly what they were cultivating. Their perplexed expressions remained as they nodded their heads in sympathetic ignorance but at least they realised that Jack and Molly were not harvesting anything illegal.

She puts a couple of stray mangos that had been lost among the sweet potatoes into the fruit bowl on the dresser. Looking up, Molly notices her reflection in the mirror. Her clear skin and the glossy nut- brown of her shoulder length hair offer few signs of aging. Jack's skeletal grin beams back at her from the photograph tucked into the bottom right-hand corner of the glass. He'd lost a lot of weight after one year of raw food and the angered response of the starved, belligerent cancer. But some of the pain had disappeared with it too.

She recalls taking the photograph at a lunch organized for close friends. While they all proffered their surprised enjoyment of the unusual array of food, they concealed their fear that Jack was killing himself. They knew they would have to be ready to support Molly in the aftermath of the tragedy that was unfolding. Evidence everywhere showed that scientifically based medical intervention was his only hope. But even Molly, who had throughout her career dismissed complementary intervention, began to doubt the science when Jack celebrated the Christmas he wasn't supposed to have seen.

She began looking at Jack's research in more depth and started to undertake some of her own investigations. She'd expected to find reams of insubstantial anecdotal evidence but was amazed by the positive factual experimental outcomes delivered in support of alternative and drug-free lifestyles. Some of the testimonials about preventing and curing cancer were astonishing. But in Molly's industry, such findings were regarded as crack-pot nonsense. Any worthwhile cure or form of pain relief required skilled enquiry and was therefore expensive, especially as individuals' dependency upon treatment was inevitably a lifelong outcome. She convinced Jack that they should write a book, sharing the substantial evidence they'd discovered, as well as their own experiences, thoughts and recipes.

'You realise we'll be challenging the motivations of the company we've worked for all these years?' he'd said.

'Oh, I know we can't make a dent in Big Pharma, Jack. But in some small way, we might encourage people to consider an alternative.'

It was just as they had finished a Radio 4 interview marking the one millionth sale of 'Live Food' when Jack collapsed in the street. It was nearly five years since his first diagnosis. She related Jack's well-rehearsed story to the paramedics as they shot through the traffic. Then, just like old times, she sat in the Oncology Department's family room staring at her cold cup of tea.

Let go if you want to, Jack, she thought, as she waited for his consultant, Mr Henderson, to deliver the news she already knew.

A thread of sunlight dances on something beneath the mirror. Molly picks up Jack's gold wristwatch and rubs her thumb across its shattered face. It had been damaged when he'd fallen on the pavement, the hands stopping at thirteen minutes past eleven. She smiles and returns it to its place next to the signed hardback copy of the first edition their book. As she does so, her mobile springs into life in her dressing gown pocket.

'Hi, love. Enjoying your day off?'

'Still in my pyjamas. How was your appointment?'

'All fine. The scar's healed nicely and no infection.'

'No other complications then?'

'None, thankfully. I bumped into Mr Henderson and we had a laugh about me ending up back here with a burst appendix. Anyway, I'll see you in about an hour. How about eating out tonight?'

Jack's name disappears on the phone. Molly sets aside the shopping list and runs upstairs to get dressed. If she's quick she can get her resignation letter into the morning post. *May as well make the evening a double celebration,* she thinks.

Lawrence Geoffrey is a dinosaur

If Lawrence Geoffrey hadn't known about the existence of dinosaurs near Preston, he may never have truly discovered himself. For many years, he directed interested parties towards a prehistoric playground of ferocious looking creatures in exchange for loads of cash. He sacrificed long hours of his life revealing this secret corner of Lancashire and people were amazed when they first heard of the site lying almost equidistant from the M6 and Blackpool. Day after day, dinosaur hunters tracked Lawrence down and he imparted the knowledge he had been given.

Lawrence never really mastered the names – Tyranno-something-or-other, Veloci-whatsit, Stego-Brachio-doodah. Dino-birds, Raptors, Ornithopods. The experts were well-versed in them and the average punter just wanted a day out or to keep the kids occupied.

Words had always been Lawrence's betrayers, his enemies. Written words let him down at every opportunity, hiding and distorting their meanings and shapes. At school, they violently fought on the page of his reading book; they scrambled on top of each other in his head and they shuddered from his pen, forming an untidy and nonsensical heap on his exam papers.

'Lawrence Thick Bonce, Lawrence Thick Bonce,' whispered the other boys like a condemning Greek Chorus.

The Headmaster of Preston Yonder Secondary Modern was glad to be rid of Lawrence. 'I've no idea how the boy is going to survive,' he told Lawrence's parents. 'He lacks aptitude and will achieve nothing. Quite frankly, he has failed the school.'

Mr. and Mrs. Geoffrey couldn't understand why their son was so daft. With a name like Lawrence, he was destined to be successful in life, surely? Mr Geoffrey's grandfather, also a Lawrence, had been awarded the Victoria Cross in the First World War and Mrs. Geoffrey had fallen in love with Lawrence of Arabia – T.E. Lawrence, so his first name was in fact Thomas but she didn't know that - as portrayed by Peter O'Toole. But with a name like Lawrence in the unexceptional town of Preston Yonder, one's destiny lay in a barrage of consistent bullying and humiliation.

Lawrence's dad owned a large garage in Preston Yonder. He'd built up the business from very little, hoping that one day the signage would read 'Geoffrey & Son'. But Lawrence was incapable of stripping a bed, let alone a car engine. Mr Geoffrey asked all his customers and contacts if they could offer Lawrence a job, any job. Most of them felt sorry for the Geoffreys, but none of them could see why anyone would choose to employ Lawrence, even as an act of charity.

Then something came up.

'I need a ticket seller,' said Nigel Smythe, the owner of the Dinosaur Invasion Park in Preston Yonder - or DIPPY, as the locals called it - and one of Mr. Geoffrey's most valued customers. 'Send Lawrence over next week and we'll try him out.'

Nigel Smythe was Preston Yonder's finest entrepreneur. He'd gone to work in London when he left school – no one was quite sure what he did but it was where he made his fortune – and returned to Preston Yonder where he bought the faded buildings of dying companies and converted them into rented storage space, industrial units and several smart housing developments. Two years ago, he bought the burgeoning business that was the Dinosaur Invasion Park in Preston Yonder and transformed it into a very successful tourist attraction.

Lawrence's parents were both delighted and concerned. 'Don't mess up this opportunity, Lawrence,' said his father at the breakfast table on Lawrence's first day. 'I can't afford to lose the DIPPY contract, OK?'

But to their amazement, Lawrence took to the job in the ticket booth as quickly as day-trippers had chosen not to visit Preston Yonder before DIPPY was revamped. His fear of the written word was abated by the colour-coded entry tickets – blue, red, green, yellow, white: family, adult, child, student, senior citizen. Nigel Smythe disliked the contemporary convention of concessions. He didn't encourage the admission of the unemployed and he resented the expensive investment he'd been legally required to make to admit the disabled with their oversized cars, carers and mobility aids.

Handling money was easy for Lawrence too; the computerized cash register did it all. And when visitors asked questions, he handed them the adventure park leaflet that contained everything they needed to know from where the toilets were to what a Megalosaurus liked to eat.

He'd watch them arrive, striding up from the car park wearing their anticipation and excitement beneath nylon waterproofs – summer in Preston Yonder was very unpredictable. Families were often led by one determined parent - the other wishing they were going to Preston Yonder's large retail village - who carried a rucksack so full of flasks, sandwiches, biscuits, binoculars, cameras, clothing and other vital equipment, it would have been comfortable on the back of a Royal Marine. As they formed a line and stopped, Lawrence would open his ticket booth window – PHWIP! - exchange the few necessary words, complete the transaction, close the booth window – PHWIP! –and that was it. Once they were through the entrance barrier, it was up to the staff in the park to guide the visitors and address any further questions or problems.

When Lawrence wasn't dealing with the public, he'd stack the torn off ticket stubs in neat colour coded piles, secured with matching rubber bands. Later, he'd watch the visitors carry their souvenirs, their sore feet and sometimes their boredom and disappointment back to the carpark. He started to draw them in a small sketchbook he kept under the cash register, finishing off his pieces in the evening at home but never showing them to anyone.

Lawrence was particularly interested in those people, male or female, young or old, who somehow stood out from the crowd. Colourful clothing, bright jewellery, a well-executed hairstyle, a good figure – they were all caught on the end or his pencil and transferred to paper. He never drew faces as so many of them looked tired and occasionally bore a downcast demeanour at the end of a long day spent in a place in which they didn't want to be. But Lawrence didn't feel sorry for them. He didn't care. He wasn't interested in dinosaurs. He wasn't really interested in people.

Mr. Smythe exchanged the same few words with him every evening when he came to close up. 'A good day's takings here, Geoffrey.'

'Yes, Mr Smythe.'

Mr. Smythe always called him Geoffrey, even after Lawrence had corrected him a few times and then had given up. Lawrence Geoffrey, Geoffrey Lawrence. He could be two people with two completely different personalities and lifestyles. Preston Yonder's very own Jekyll and Hyde.

After finishing work at 5.00pm, Lawrence cycled straight home to have tea with his parents. Mr and Mrs Geoffrey had an active social life in Preston Yonder, attending dances, bridge games, and rotary, freemason and church events. Lawrence looked forward to these occasions when he was alone in the house. Otherwise, they would all watch his father's favourite television programmes with Lawrence enduring derogative remarks whenever a successful business tycoon or action man was eulogizing.

'Look, Lawrence. That could have been you if only you'd applied yourself.'

His parents had never understood him. They stopped asking him what he did on his day off.

'I'm just going out and about,' was all he'd say.

But for Lawrence, his day off was when he could indulge in his secret. He loved colour and he loved to draw. In primary school he'd covered pages of his exercise books with brightly coloured pictures when they should have recorded his times tables. The creative crime issued an artful punishment from a cruel teacher which suppressed Lawrence's passion until it had re-emerged in the sketches done in the safety of the ticket booth.

Sharing his secret or anything else was out of the question. Sharing special things only resulted in pain and humiliation.

On his weekly day off from DIPPY, Lawrence sat alone in the reference section at the local library. He'd gone in there for the first time on a very wet day when he'd forgotten his umbrella. The condensation on his glasses had left him wandering among the shelves, feeling anxious to be surrounded by so many books and words.

The mist cleared and Lawrence found himself staring at beautiful illustrations and photographs in an exhibition of enormous art books. From that moment he started to systematically work his way through the dusty shelves in the art section, losing himself in portraits, landscapes, fabrics, costumes, ceramics, sculptures, photographs, abstracts.

Even the accompanying words were beginning to make more sense. But it was the visual delights that leapt from every page and spoke to him like old friends. He could read the emotions in these books: beauty, ugliness, happiness, sadness, humour, anger, sorrow. Lawrence spent hours carefully and precisely copying pictures into notebooks which he hid under the floorboards beneath his bed.

A heavy slate-grey January sky was pressing against the library window when Lawrence opened a large volume containing page after page of elaborate operatic costumes. He was struck by the brilliance of the women's outfits: huge, colourful ballgowns with rivers of silk skirts, pinched waists, vast peacock feathers, delicately intricate shoes, lavish jewels, exquisite arrays of hats, gloves, handbags, flowing capes, parasols...

On and on, they revealed themselves to Lawrence, who could almost sense the array of textures beneath his trembling fingers. Lawrence was more excited by these images than anything he'd ever seen, copying and sketching until the librarian, who enjoyed the quiet company of her weekly visitor, reluctantly asked him to leave at closing time.

Lawrence's life at work and at home unfolded without incident but now he had so much more to muse over during the dull daytime hours in his fibreglass cocoon. He tried to compare the dishcloth-toned women who ambled past his booth with the gregarious costumes in his notebook. No comparison.

Six work days of magnificent images in his head and six late nights staring at the sketches hidden in his bedroom carried him through to his weekly trip to the library. He left the house before his mother cooked breakfast and sat outside the sturdy Victorian building waiting for it to open. Mrs Geoffrey, who was honestly pleased not to have Lawrence at home all day, happened to mention his peculiar behaviour to her husband. She thought nothing of it but he decided to do some investigative work. He discovered from the librarian's father, a fellow Rotarian, where Lawrence was spending his day off. Mr. Geoffrey confronted his son.

'A bit late now isn't it, wasting your time with books?'

'But I think I've found a way to ...'

'I thought you could help your mother with the housework but she said no ...

'... something that could really ...'

'... so, I've organized some golf lessons for you next week.'

'... that I really enjoy.'

'Time you joined the club. Time you joined in generally.'

'Dad, I don't think I ...'

'And I've had a chat with Nigel. Your day off is Wednesday from now on.'

Wednesday. The day when the library was closed.

As well as being a respectable community figure in Preston Yonder, where he'd been born, Lawrence's dad was the embodiment of the alpha male – hardworking at his own business during the week, a few pints on Friday night, football on Saturday, golf with the lads on Sunday. He'd never been able to persuade his son to partake in any of these pursuits and he blamed himself for being too soft on the lad. He should never have listened to his wife's protestations about their son's 'difficulties'. She'd always been far too overprotective, he thought, and now something had to change before Lawrence became more embarrassing than Mr Geoffrey could cope with.

So here was Lawrence on Wednesday morning at the driving range. The golf lessons didn't get off to a good start when the golf pro, Alan, who'd been two years ahead of Lawrence at school, could only find an antiquated, rusty and slightly bent practice set of left-handed clubs for his client. Alan hated teaching the southpaws, believing beyond all doubt that they were cack-handed, clumsy and lacked coordination.

Lawrence spent two mornings swiping, slicing and chopping the air around him. Things looked promising when he hit the ball off the tee three times, even if it did only travel ten feet. From all the other practice stands came the sound of crack and whoosh as driving irons made contact with golf balls that shot effortlessly into the air and travelled many yards in a beautifully-arced trajectory. When Lawrence accidentally let go of one of the clubs so that it smashed through the closed window of the Management office, narrowly missing the cleaner, Alan decided to have a discreet word with Lawrence's father.

Mr. Geoffrey insisted that Alan should persevere with the lessons, offering free MOTs and services indefinitely and then threatening to report Alan to the club captain. But Alan knew that wouldn't go anywhere and he remained politely defiant.

'I'm sorry, Mr. Geoffrey but there's nothing I can do for Lawrence's handicap.'

A heart attack at the 13th hole put an end to Mr Geoffrey's club membership and to his life. This was followed, six months later, by Mrs Geoffrey's death. A broken heart, the neighbours said. Couldn't face the rest of her days looking after her miserable son, others said. But Lawrence appeared neither miserable nor happy. He'd lived, but not really lived, with his parents for such a long time that there wasn't a strong familial tie waiting to be torn apart. He missed the things that Mrs Geoffrey had done for him but Lawrence adapted domestic life to suit him. He accepted Nigel Smythe's paltry offer for the garage on the day he scattered his parents' ashes under a tree they'd donated to The Rotary Club Memorial Garden.

Now Lawrence was comfortable with a home, a job and microwave meals. His reading had improved since he'd left school but he didn't trust his ability. At the Citizens Advice Bureau, Lawrence lied about losing his glasses and persuaded a smiling, grey-haired gentleman volunteer to help him transfer bills and other paperwork into his name and to show him how to pay off the mortgage. He was surprised at how much he was able to understand but didn't let on to the volunteer. Lawrence returned home with a degree of confidence that he'd never felt before and was worthy of the box of jam doughnuts he'd bought at the bakery.

Just before the twentieth anniversary of his arrival at DIPPY, Lawrence got a new boss. Nigel Smythe retired and Nigel Junior took over. He was a more amiable man than his father, seeking the approval of his employees while recognising that they knew how to run things and would not welcome change. Nigel Junior, unlike his father, did not have lots of other business interests, and consequently spent most of his days either in his DIPPY office or walking the grounds of the theme park.

The staff weren't too keen on Nigel Junior's presence. They were used to running the park their way – and to their advantage - and without the interference of Nigel Senior whom they kept happy and at arm's length with a show of healthy profits. Nigel Junior struggled with their reticence and was relieved to find what he believed to be an ally in Lawrence.

They were a similar age, although Nigel Junior had been sent away to boarding school rather than attend the local comprehensive. He enjoyed talking at length to Lawrence each day. Lawrence didn't say much in return. He didn't need to as his opinion was rarely sought – something he'd grown accustomed to with his parents - and his new boss obviously loved the sound of his own voice.

Lawrence had less time to sketch but it was a small sacrifice to make for his new boss. Nigel Junior had, after all, changed his day off back to a Tuesday and never referred to him as Geoffrey.

Without the suffocating presence of his parents, Lawrence had developed another new interest. It had started innocently as all these things do: changing into his mother's clothes in the evening when he returned from work. He'd shared all his father's rather dull overcoats, suits, shirts, ties and shoes among the town's charity shops. He'd even seen a few men wearing some of the items, appearing like ghostly apparitions in front of him on the High Street. But when Lawrence had opened his mother's wardrobe, he'd been astounded by what hung before him.

The padded hangers displayed evening and cocktail dresses, blouses, soft cardigans, jumpers. Beneath them stood several rows of shoes for all kinds of occasions. Lawrence struggled to find an image of her wearing these beautiful things but nothing emerged from his memory. He'd simply never paid her much attention, always in his room when she'd called up the stairs to say goodbye on her way out to some local function with his father. His sketchbooks full of costume drawings seemed lifeless now that he could touch and smell these beautiful clothes.

Lawrence searched through the wardrobe, pushing hangers along the rail with increasing excitement, and pulling out various garments to examine them more closely before discarding them on his parents' bed. When he'd finished, he turned to look at the large collection draped across the duvet. His heart battered at his ribcage and his breathing quickened. Lawrence just wanted to try on everything. He selected a purple silk knee-length cocktail dress and so his escape into his own fantasy world began.

On that first occasion, the thrill and elation were so overwhelming for Lawrence that he could try on no more than six dresses. He was surprised at how well they fitted him, having never considered for one moment that he shared the same slight build as his mother. The material caressed his skin and comforted him, sending a rush of exhilaration through his veins that seemed to awaken his entire being. As Lawrence gazed at his reflection in the mirror, he liked the look of the person who was smiling at him from across the room.

It was the librarian who first noticed the change in Lawrence's demeanour. It wasn't a seismic shift, and initially, she couldn't clearly identify it. There was something about the way he walked over to the art books that was different, a more erect posture, a lighter step. She knew why he came to the library, week after week, and she'd endeavour to get a glimpse of his work when he took a toilet break.

She was astonished by the richness and detail of his sketches and a little sad that the skill he had acquired through hours of practice and application remained undiscovered. But she couldn't say anything to him as it would reveal her betrayal of his trust. He even smiled at her, saying hello and goodbye as he entered and exited the building every Tuesday, behaviour that, from Lawrence, she was unaccustomed to.

He wasn't any more talkative at work but began to occasionally wave at some of the staff and visitors as they passed his booth. They waved back, their mood subconsciously lifted to a brighter place for a brief moment. No one questioned the small transformation of Lawrence Geoffrey. They just reckoned he'd put his grief behind him and learned to take care of himself. But for Lawrence, it was the daily anticipation of visiting the safety of his other world every evening along with the uninterrupted exploration of his art that was preventing his stagnation and moving him forward.

One Saturday night, exhausted from an unusually busy week at work and a long session of trying to complete a self-portrait, Lawrence, dressed in a full-length crimson taffeta ballgown with puffball sleeves and a netted underskirt, slid into his mother's armchair. He kicked off the matching high heels decorated with tiny sequins and gently smoothed down the full skirt.

Lawrence turned on the television and flicked through the channels. The remote control offered up a long stream of programmes, most of them unfamiliar to Lawrence as he'd watched very little television since his mother's death. A particular image caused his thumb to hit the Select button. Lawrence leaned forward, the fitted bodice squeezing his waist and ribs, and stared at the man being interviewed. He didn't take in anything that was being said. Instead, Lawrence was mesmerised by what the man was wearing: a white leather mini-skirt and jacket and matching knee-high boots with six-inch heels.

But it was the make-up and jewellery, revealed by a camera close-up, that caused Lawrence's mouth to open wide. He watched the entire documentary as it addressed the issues and concerns of transsexuals and cross-dressers. Lawrence nodded in agreement with many of the things that were said: how most of the men didn't want to be women but they enjoyed the sensation of wearing women's clothes and that they felt able to express themselves and manage stress through cross-dressing.

'That is me, that is me', Lawrence whispered at the screen. *There is nothing wrong with me.* He was fascinated by all the participants, both men and women, although he was never quite sure who was what as their outfits, styled wigs, painted faces and polished nails were so convincingly breath-taking. Lawrence cried as he observed the kindred spirits on the screen. He went to bed longing to be among them.

There was a small nightclub in Preston Yonder called Crossed Out. He'd discovered it on his way home from buying a Saturday night take away fish supper. This was a recent change of routine and it had introduced him to a queue of extraordinary looking people similar to those he'd watched in the documentary: men like women, women like men, all happily chatting and waiting for the doors to open.

Throughout the following week he had a powerful urge to join them but doubted whether he could actually do it. What would he wear? What would he say if anyone spoke to him? He sifted through all his mother's clothes several times and finally chose a red silk tunic dress and matching shoes. For once in his life, Lawrence was grateful to be small-framed and skinny. He applied full make up, following instructions he'd found in a magazine, and one of his mother's brunette wigs from her amateur dramatic pursuits. *I'll need to buy a selection of these for future occasions*, he thought to himself. A sable fur coat and soft leather handbag completed the ensemble and off he went.

No one questioned his appearance in the queue. He blended in with the delicious synthesis of humanity. Once inside, he bought a lemonade – Lawrence didn't drink alcohol – and marvelled at the luxurious and colourful décor as well as the broad array of customers. A few people smiled and said hello. Lawrence's voice had deserted him and he could only smile back.

He found a dimly lit corner of the bar where he could tuck himself away and be a silent and invisible observer. Lawrence was loving every minute of it, content to be part of the crowd, content not to have to speak to anyone. When he stood up to adjust his dress and buy another drink, a hand stroked his bottom and a hot, whispery hello tickled his ear.

Lawrence turned around to face Nigel Smythe Junior. Instantaneously, two lip-sticked smiles evaporated as two pairs of eyes, discernible beneath shimmering eye shadow, liner and mascara, assimilated what was before them. Each man silently spoke the other one's name, before Nigel stepped back and disappeared into the cavernous oblivion.

The magic had evaporated for Lawrence once he'd been recognised. He left the nightclub and walked home, finding the shadows to disappear into as his level of self-consciousness rose. In his bedroom, he pulled off the dress and wig and, seated at his mother's dressing table, started to remove the make-up.

As he wiped away the layers, he was reminded of a picture of the sad-looking clown, from the opera *Pagliacci*, that he had drawn in his sketchbook. He stared at his smeared reflection and asked it why Nigel had touched him. Up until that moment, he'd felt so safe and at home in the nightclub but his boss's actions had made him want to wash and scrub himself away, to erase his existence. The person watching him in the mirror did not have an answer.

He'd drifted through Sunday, his mood a volley of mild anxiety and cautious excitement, knowing that he and Nigel must have something in common. He didn't fancy Nigel – he'd never been attracted to anyone and that suited him. No, it wasn't anything like that. Lawrence was sure they could settle that misunderstanding.

When Lawrence entered his ticket booth on Monday morning, Nigel was waiting for him. There'd been a discrepancy in the accounts which had been traced back to ticket sales, apparently. The company would rectify this but Lawrence no longer had a job. Nigel said he was sorry to have to let Lawrence go under these circumstances but the restructuring-modernisation-need-for-new-blood-and-a-fresh-approach was also inevitable and there'd be no place for him at DIPPY. Lawrence stared at the bulging brown envelope Nigel had just given him.

'I don't understand, Mr Smythe. I've never made a mistake.'

'Just take the money and bugger off, you little pervert,' hissed Nigel. 'And remember to keep your mouth shut, if you know what's good for you.'

Nigel need not have worried. Lawrence knew nothing about workplace rights and duly accepted his pay off. He would have been happy to keep Nigel's secret, to be his friend.

Lawrence went home and put on his mother's favourite midnight-blue evening dress with matching full-length gloves. He had a rare recollection of her looking incredibly stunning when she wore it to the Rotary Club Christmas Dinner. He got into bed with his sketchbooks and slowly began to tear and shred page after page. Now there was nowhere for him to go in this world. For the first time in his life, as he contemplated his extinction, Lawrence learned something about dinosaurs.

The women who lost their resolve

Monday morning. Connie sat in the crowded waiting room staring at the number 666 on the orange ticket she was clutching. She wasn't superstitious. Nor was she someone who placed any faith in society's rules, its accepted norms and certainly not in faith itself. But she'd never been here before.

Connie looked at the receptionist she'd reported to earlier. Her expensively cut and styled blonde hair, her flawless make-up, her immaculately polished nails and her finely sculpted figure confirmed to Connie that she was a Resolute. She'd smiled at and even spoken to the Resolute when she'd signed in. But the Resolute had just pointed to the ticket collection machine and then to a seat.

Connie now looked at the people who'd joined her. They were a random collection of women, a cross-section of life outside the room. She'd tried chatting to her neighbours, receiving whispered, monosyllabic replies. Everyone seemed nervous and no one wanted to talk. In the end, Connie gave up and read her book in the silent gloom.

A door marked 'Female Investigation Unit' opened. Ten people walked through the doorway and into the waiting room. Two women were crying, while the faces of the others ranged from glowering red to despondent grey. None of them spoke as they stood in line at reception. Each one held a card ready for presentation to the Resolute who didn't appear to be programmed with a personality. A second Resolute stood by the open door and shouted at the waiting women.

'Numbers 661 to 700. Show me your tickets as you enter.'

143

The shouting Resolute was a replica of the reception Resolute, except for her short black hair. Connie had laughed at the rumours of Officialdom cloning but now she wasn't so sure. Women stood up, collecting bags and coats. A few returned magazines to the small table in the centre of the room. The Resolute continued shouting. 'Hurry up. This is a busy time of year and there are lots of confessions to be processed.'

The air in the small, white investigation room tasted clinical. A tiny window framing a rain-cloud sky was made redundant by harsh, bright lighting. The women stood behind cold metal chairs arranged in a circle. One chair was empty.

'I need to go and find a missing file,' shouted the Resolute. 'We'll start the confessions when I return.' She stopped by the door and turned her perfect gaze on the group. 'No talking until then.'

She was met with silence. 'Do you understand?'

Connie could see the faint look of disgust in the eyes of the Resolute.

'We understand,' they all replied. All except Connie, who winked and gave a thumbs up to the CCTV after the Resolute had slammed the door.

The women sat down, avoiding eye contact. Connie counted to ten, by which time she was bursting to speak. 'OK, ladies, I'll tell you why I'm here.'

'You can't,' whispered a large woman looking uncomfortable in a purple lycra gym kit and pink trainers. 'She told us not to.'

'That's right,' said a small woman who seemed unable to control her fidgeting hands.

'Anyway, we know why you're here,' said another woman who was struggling to sit upright in her chair. 'You've broken your resolutions. You're just like me. No guts or backbone.'

'On New Year's Eve, I promised to do more exercise, eat better and lose weight,' said Lycra Woman. 'But the credit card bill for Christmas arrived and I needed a double vodka and Death by Chocolate Cake, not a bloody kettlebell workout.'

'That was probably Blue Monday,' said a woman who constantly texted or emailed without looking up from her iPhone. 'I'd resolved to get a new job but I missed a crucial interview that day because I had to sort out another of my boss's cock-ups. Didn't get home until midnight and didn't make it to parents' evening again.'

'Welcome to the club,' said Posture-Challenged Woman, who seemed to be sliding from her chair and towards the floor.

Fidgety Woman stood up. 'Does anyone mind if I smoke?'

'Let me guess,' said Connie, who was now more interested in hearing what these women had to say rather than make her own confession. 'You promised to give up the cigarettes but it's not working out. Am I right?'

Connie watched Fidgety Woman open a battered tobacco tin with her yellow fingers and remove a roll-up. She lit the cigarette and her muscles visibly relaxed after the first inhalation. 'I didn't even leave the starting blocks, love. I know I should do it, but I lost my willpower years ago, the same time my boy disappeared.' The women sensed that there was probably no hope for her.

A tall, elegantly dressed young woman stood up. 'Mummy believes I can't stick to my resolution because I lack staying power, strength of character and a mind of my own.'

'And do you have a mind of your own?' asked iPhone Woman.

'But of course I have a mind of my own! Who else would it belong to?'

'And what was your resolution?' asked Connie.

'Well, it was really Mummy's idea. I didn't want to disappoint her and I couldn't think of anything myself.'

'So, what did you promise?' asked Lycra Woman as she took the wrapper off a chocolate protein bar.

'That this year I would persist in making new friends and find myself a husband.'

'But that takes time,' said Connie. 'You can't possibly have broken that resolution yet.'

'The thing is, I made a wonderful friend at the Tennis Club's New Year party. Now we're in love and want to get married.'

'So why on earth are you here?' asked Fidgety Woman as she stubbed her cigarette out in the Resolute's bone china tea cup.

'My new friend's name is Alison.'

Connie turned to the remaining women to establish what their lack of determination, persistence and general pluckiness had led to. A woman wearing a floor-length velvet coat spoke. 'I'm a composer of atonal music but my publisher has long been complaining that there isn't a great market for it. I therefore courageously promised to write a piece where all discordant sound resolved to concordant sound during the course of the changing harmony.'

'I see,' said Connie, who obviously did not.

Composer Woman sprang up from her chair. 'But the resolution from dominant to tonic was just too much to ask and I couldn't do it!'

'Okay, okay, anyone else?' asked Connie, before the room was subjected to further musical analysis.

'I've lost all clarity, sharpness, focus, precision and visibility.'

The women looked around the circle trying to locate the quiet voice. Then Connie noticed a pair of short legs jutting out from beneath a large television screen. She'd assumed it was part of the equipment used during the confessions.

'I'm sorry, did you say something?' Connie asked the screen.

The voice from the television continued. 'The repair man said my resolution was buggered and that I should come here for help.'

'Oh, I can sympathise with you,' said iPhone Woman. 'The resolution on my integrated camera just isn't good enough.'

'Now hold on,' said Connie. I'm not sure a telly on the blink is why' -

'Well, I'm here because the motion I proposed on equal pay at my last union meeting didn't get to a vote and couldn't be formally expressed in a resolution,' said a woman in work overalls.

'Yes, but'-

'My life is in ruins!' shouted another woman who fell to her knees beside Posture-Challenged Woman who was now lying on the floor. 'I'm poet-in-residence at the university but I'm no longer capable of the sweet, gradual resolution of an uncertain feeling into any kind of named emotion, let alone my art!'

Everyone except Connie was now talking about their resolution confessions, handing out tissues, placing consoling arms around each other, offering advice and guessing what their penalties might be for breaking the rules. Connie was reminded of the conflict resolution course she attended at work last year but decided now was not the time to draw on this experience.

She stood on her chair to speak. It took three attempts to get the women's attention. 'Stop this, everyone, please stop!'

The room gradually became silent again, apart from the drum-roll of rain on the window.

'Not one of us should be here,' said Connie. 'We haven't done anything wrong.'

'Why are you here, then?' asked Fidgety Woman as she lit another cigarette. 'What resolution did you break?'

Connie stared at the CCTV. 'I'm here because I didn't resolve to do or change something. Instead, I resolved to have something for myself.'

'What?' said Lycra Woman, sipping an energy drink. 'That doesn't make sense. It's got to be something you must do, whether you like it or not.'

Posture-Challenged Woman agreed. 'I've spent years working my way through the official New Year Resolution list and failed at everything. Why do you think I look like this?'

'Because you've been made to think you're a loser, a failure,' Connie replied. 'I challenge you to accept yourself for who you are and walk out of this room.'

'But what did you resolve to have?' asked Television Woman who had emerged from behind her screen.

'More of what I've already got,' said Connie.

Poet Woman looked excited. 'Inspirational! Do continue. I think I can use this.'

'OK. I made a promise to myself to have more fun, more money, more sex...

'I'd definitely like some more of that,' said New Year Party woman.

'...more time with my family...'

'That's really why I wanted a new job,' said iPhone Woman as she switched off her device.

'...but also, more time for myself, more friends, more holidays.'

'Now hang on a minute,' said Lycra Woman. 'Isn't that just plain greed?'

'No, I'm just being honest about what I want to have and then I'll decide what I need to do to achieve it.'

'And what makes you so different from the rest of us?' asked Composer Woman.

'You've all made the mistake of compiling a to do list based on the social narrative of what is expected of you.' Connie looked at Television Woman then Overall Woman. 'Well, some of you have.'

Lycra Woman looked perplexed. 'And in plain English that means exactly what?'

'That we and no one else may decide how to live our lives,' said Posture-Challenged Woman as she stood up.

Connie jumped down from the chair. 'Exactly! Now, I'm a scientist and in physics, the method of resolution occurs when a single force is replaced by two or more jointly equivalent to it.'

'So what?' mumbled Fidgety Woman as she offered her cigarettes around.

Connie smiled and pointed at the door. 'How about we test the method on the Resolute when she returns?'

Where Fortunes Lie

Moira Harris

Moira Harris enjoyed a fulfilling career as a professional singer and voice teacher. She moved from London to the Scottish Highlands where she now pursues her interests as a writer and artist. When she's not in her creative cave, Moira will be walking the hills, backpacking, cycling and seeking adventures and experiences in her beloved motor-home.